Saeeda's Trinity

Jack M. Barrack Hebrew Academy

Saeeda's Trinity

From Precious To Provocative Novel

Dr. David Rabeeya

Copyright © 2009 by Dr. David Rabeeya.

Library of Congress Control Number: 2009903802
ISBN: Softcover   978-1-4415-2965-7

All rights reserved. No part of this book may be reproduced or transmitted in any form or by any means, electronic or mechanical, including photocopying, recording, or by any information storage and retrieval system, without permission in writing from the copyright owner.

This is a work of fiction. Names, characters, places and incidents either are the product of the author's imagination or are used fictitiously, and any resemblance to any actual persons, living or dead, events, or locales is entirely coincidental.

This book was printed in the United States of America.

To order additional copies of this book, contact:
Xlibris Corporation
1-888-795-4274
www.Xlibris.com
Orders@Xlibris.com

This book is dedicated to all Jews who were born in Arab lands for their resilience and strength in facing their challenges, tragedies and loss.

I wish to thank Arlene again for her incredible support. A special thank you to Jane Schofer for the editorial work and Valerie Linden for typing the material. Without their help this book would not be possible.

PART I

Saeeda's Trinity

From Precious to Provocative Novel

By Dr. David Rabeeya

CHAPTER 1

She was spoiled and she knew it. She memorized all of the flowery Arabic compliments which were bestowed upon her by her parents. Words like "princess", "Allah's gift" and the "smartest of all" had often rung in her ears. Her mother frequently reminded her that her name Saeeda meant "joy" and she needed to prove her name with her beliefs and deeds. She loved the Arabic language and wrote poems in it about the Almighty Allah and her expectations for a future handsome husband. With her parents, she saw movies starring Hollywood's male stars and in her mind, a man similar to them in fame and beauty would ask for her hand.

Her father worked with the British administration of Iraq. He was well-to do, respected, and, the most important thing, he spoiled her to death. She never asked him the reason for being an only child while all of her neighbors had at least nine children. She liked it this way. All attention was given to her. Life was beyond wonderful. Life was magical. In her high school for girls, only she excelled in Arabic and French. She was often praised by her female teachers for her dedication to her studies, her charm and her maturity. She was always first in her class, always at the center of attention. However, she never overstated her success. Many of her friends loved her company even as they often envied her and gossiped behind her back. "Girls giggle and talk a lot," she explained, "It's nothing serious. There is no harm in a little silly talk."

On her birthdays, her parents used to invite Iraqi singers with their oods, their doombegs and their fiddles to sing songs in her honor. Her relatives and friends were invited. Men danced with women. With a little Aqaq booze, the two genders mixed nicely. One of her favorite songs was the one that ends with the words "May Allah repeat their joy again." Her father took her to the famous shorja market to buy her more jewelry for these rewarding occasions. She wore golden necklaces and silver rings and her lips now had a touch of reddish color which accentuated her brown beauty. Her mother used black pencil to paint her eyelashes which had opened the eyes of those young men around her.

In her place, sex was not discussed publicly. She heard everything from her mother and when the blood appeared for her the first time, her mother hugged her and called her a "mara" (woman). She told her that Allah was pleased with her because life was running in her private parts. Saeeda was excited, confused, happy and concerned. "Her mother was wonderful and sensitive," she thought. She told her that her father would love her now even more because sooner or later she would bear children and make him grandsons and granddaughters. Their butlers, Sami and Hakima, were always ready to please her and her parents, but her mother told her not to talk to them or to anyone about her bloody spots. She would only tell her father to bring joy to his male heart. Nevertheless, Saeeda was compelled to tell her secrets to some of her female friends because they told her about their mixed blessings and physical adventures.

She loved King Feisal, the Second with his British dress and his marvelous hat with feathers of color. He was so young and innocent like her. He was always smiling and cheerful. She stood with her parents when she was a toddler at the beginning of movies that she watched. They saluted him with a military salute while the Iraqi flag with its anthem was scattered on the screen. Saeeda was convinced that the world of childhood was nothing but a serene movie with unending laughter, fun and imaginative games. After all, several times a year she went on the bus on a tour outside of Baghdad to see the wonders of those who had created her civilization. She was told that she was not far from the Garden of Eden and very close to the walls of Hammurabi. In the national museum, she saw the statues of Assyrian horses with their wings and the restored jars with Acadian scripts.

She was a child of the past and present. She was, in her teenage mind, the mystery of days which will never be returned and the actual days of her everyday life. Her father always encouraged her to read, to listen to the radio and to read the paper. She quickly realized that there were many poor people around her and her residence in the exclusive sector of Baghdad was a great privilege by God's gift.

Surprisingly, rumors had spread in her school about attempts by generals in the army to assassinate her beloved king, but Saeeda was like many of her age, concentrating on herself alone. Being narcissistic and selfish were virtues she wrote about in one of her poems. She only smiled when she wrote: "I wish to be for myself for a long time because I do not have a specific agenda like adults." She chuckled after she completed writing these words with her special fountain pen with pure blue ink which resided on her neat desk in her highly decorated room.

Her parents made connections with the famous publisher known as Al-Quala in the noisy capital. They praised her profound thoughts and her incredible richness of rhythms and rhymes. They emphasized both her admiration of the king and her insights into the human soul. Saeeda knew that many of her peers had tried the craft of Arabic verse but she convinced herself that she was among the best—or at least higher than average. She called her collections of poems Rabii (my spring). She wrote about her love of God, her parents and her friends. Her words were both sharp in their naiveté and profound in their reflections. Her family name was Baghdadi and in her society, this name could not reveal her ethnic or religious affiliation. It was safe in this way. In the literary section of the famous Al-Zaman paper, the editor offered many accolades to her linguistic genius and her pure thoughts. "Life was the ultimate thing," she said.

Some of her girlfriends, who were living the good life, came to see her to do homework together and to listen to the voice of the Eastern singing star, Oom-Kalthoom. Saeeda loved Iraqi music in the same way as the air she breathed, but she was like others, mesmerized by the sound of the Egyptian singer. After all, two extended things existed forever and ever: the pyramids and the divine voice of Oom-Kalthoom. She was an unattractive woman, fat and full of flesh, but when she began to sing, millions of Arabs surrendered to her shrieking, emotionally sincere voice. Saeeda spent hours listening to the heavenly sounds which came out of the mouth of this singer who sang about faith, suffering and redemption. Everyone was talking about about her. Saeeda was often in tears just listening to the words of this magical Egyptian personality.

Saeeda read books on philosophy, history and religion, but she did not neglect to feed her emotional soul with the struggle and pain of others who faced defeats and trials. She was extra sensitive but she did not have hysterical attacks. Saeeda spent hours looking at her grown body. Her nipples had grown from tiny nuts to full pomegranates. Her lips had broadened in her beauty at last. Her lower body began to be similar to a precious guitar in its form. Her black hair grew backwards and reached down to her behind which added considerable attraction to her physique.

Saeeda's mother was working in a nearby British bank. It was part time work because she needed time to keep an eye on the cook to make sure his food would be delicious. She gave orders to the domestics and they were always thankful for her generosity. She was a kind person in the eyes of many. Giving charity was in her blood. Saeeda told stories upon stories about the way her mother met her father. How her mother was poor and thin, thrown in the street after the death of her parents. How her father saw her and loved her in a minute. Saeeda loved to tell real and not so real stories about the romance of her parents. Saeeda liked to dream and she loved when she lost herself in the imaginative world of her youth. She sometimes prayed her own personal prayers and she felt that her personal God was paying attention to her requests.

Conversations on the phone were very popular in those days. Her father asked her not to keep the line busy for a long time, but with her feminine smile she convinced him to surrender his anger at the door.

Saeeda was shocked when she heard about the hanging of three youths her age due to their membership in the illegal Communist party. However, her stream of life continued undisturbed. Volunteers had demonstrated in the street and the police opened fire and killed tens of them but her parents were not extremely concerned. They did not belong to any political party. They were Iraqi patriots. They were loyal to the kingdom. "There is nothing to worry about," she was told.

CHAPTER 2

He stood on the corners of Rasheed Street warning people about the end of the world. Saeeda saw him often but only left a few coins in his basket. He had long and messy hair, he never shaved, and his clothes were dirty and torn. Her parents criticized those children who threw stones at him and spat in his face for fun. "It is unacceptable," she was told, "to behave to God's creatures in a cruel fashion." Allah is writing in his book all of the sins of each human being and those nutty teenagers will pay the price in the hereafter. Saeeda knew that there is reward and punishment and that nothing is missed by the guy in heaven. She took these matters seriously. "Did he watch her when she examined her body in front of the mirror? Would she be punished for cursing eloquently with sexual innuendo in Arabic? Is it possible that Allah will reward her parents with a long life because of their contributions to the weak?"

Units of the Iraqi Army were moving to Palestine. Why? The government proclaimed war against the enemies of Iraq. In school, nationalist students began singing patriotic songs about sacrifice, death and destruction. Saeeda's parents hired three body guards for themselves and her. However, she continued to get into a boat on the Tigris, fishing and then cooking and eating the delicious bodies of the sweet fish. Campfires continued to be lit in order to cook the flesh of the fish. Nights on the Tigris with the breeze and the altars in the sky were incredibly impressive. This Iraq, with its beauty, could penetrate the bones of those who were lucky to be born there.

Allah was so generous with Mesopotamian Iraq. He gave her plenty of waters, huge amounts of oil, fruit, vegetables and plenty of dates, milk and yogurt; the desert in the East, the mountains in the north, hot temperatures and the cool winds of Kurdistan. Nothing was missing. Saeeda often blessed the Almighty God for his incredible love of her country.

On the other side, tanks were visible in the streets with their menacing cannons. A military regime was declared again. Troops were sent to fight the proud Kurds of the high mountains. They had never surrendered to the king. They had never given up their fight in the snowy hills. Saeeda was amazed by the continuous tenacity and strength of these Kurds to achieve equality with their Arab neighbors. They loved their oil, their language and their power and they died to preserve them.

Saeeda knew the geography of Iraq because her parents had spent the tough high summer in Basra. Basra had received the cool breeze from the Gulf and the date trees had offered delicious dessert and cakes. In Northern Mosul, they rented a house, a palace, and enjoyed relaxing walks on the paths of the handsome mountains. From time to time, shots were heard in the distance but Saeeda convinced herself that people were only shooting pigeons for food. Saeeda continued to see children jumping from the high bridge over the river. These were children who jumped because of bets placed on them between Iraqi soldiers. If the came back up, they would get part of the bet money. However, many never did come up again. The merchants continued to shout that their merchandise was a bargain. The coffee houses continued to hear the sounds of the games shesh-besh and dominos with minty sugary tea in the background.

"Life was an Iraqi life," Saeeda concluded. There was tranquility on the surface but flowing, angry, lava below. It was a time to celebrate the peaceful time, the richness of family and her unlimited privileges. Violence and conflict could wait. Our king would not allow these to develop into anarchy. Saeeda was busy taking lessons on the piano. Life could wait. The Darwish, (Dervish) that ragged fellow who stood begging on the corners, continued to predict the arrival of black clouds. He begged for money and food and sang his rhythmic chants about the unavoidable punishment by the stars of corrupt people on earth. Saeeda feared him but she ignored him like others once shehad placed coins in his dirty basket. Somebody in their neighborhood was of interest to the secret police. It was the Darwish. He was led away with chains around his neck. Saeeda watched but she continued to dance the dances of the proceeding spring with her female friends

Yet, her father began to stay at home after work. Visitors rarely came to see her family but the pleasant life and luxury inside the spacious home continued to flourish. Exhibitions of fashion from France and England were shown in various museums but her family had decided to travel only by car with their loyal armed driver. Some bodies were seen floating in the river. Some spies were shot publicly in the football fields but the family's food was abundant and fresh. New telephones and electric lines were installed and the first television sets were placed in the royal palace. Indians and Pakistanis with their native dress continued to clean the streets and collect the garbage. The radio continued to make generous statements about his majesty, the benevolent ruler. Life was totally normal.

CHAPTER 3

The Earth Opened her Mouth

Her uncle Saleem had been arrested this morning. "Why? Where? For what?" She loved Uncle Saleem because he reminded her of her father. He had the habit of cracking jokes about everyone and everything. He also saw the absurdity of humanity. He invented stories to demonstrate the stupidity and backwardness of people. He laughed at himself, the government and the army. Saeeda knew that Arabic had charm but also an eloquence which can run away from reality. Her father warned Uncle Saleem several times that a sense of humor is not a gift, not with the rise of Arab nationalism and the declared war against the young Jewish State. Saeeda could not understand how people could kill people, how neighbor could turn against neighbor in seconds.

Her parents took the silence as a remedy in changing times. In her school, there were Jews, Armenians, Christians and Muslims. They got along fine. Some teasing about other people's religion was always in the air but nothing really alarming. All religious holidays were mentioned at their times and this was the end of it.

Suddenly, agitators arrived from outside of the school walls. They were shouting slogans against Zionism, Communism, Socialism and they were calling for Arabs to be proud and strong. Some even suggested making Islam the religion of all Iraqis. Saeeda had heard about the Promised Land and the Messiah from her parents but she was immersed in the secular European languages and the culture of the Arabs. Her parents went to the Sla (synagogue) infrequently—it was never at the center of their routine.

Muslims and Christians often came to her family's lavish parties. They served non-Kosher foods. Her family visited the powerful among the ministers, but their bodyguard decided to resign. A military regime was declared again. Special courts were summoned. In minutes, the fates of many were decided by eager, loyal judges. Thousands were arrested. Tens were executed. Hundreds were tortured. Saeeda continued to write poems about brotherhood, sisterhood and peace. She was aware of the changes but was able to deny them like most teenagers. She watched her parents sending gold and jewelry in an envelope to Iran. Her father gave the chief master of the post office a bribe to close his eyes to this smuggling scheme. "Baksheesh is always useful," Saeeda concluded.

Suspicious voices outside their home were heard. Rumors about spying on citizens were all over the city. The Chief Rabbi called all Jews to demonstrate in the streets and to shout their loyalty to Iraq and denounce Zionism. Saeeda with emotion, devotion and dedication volunteered to lead her class in Arabic slogans. She wrote statements about mother Iraq, about Jews being Arab first and Jewish second. Saeeda was asking herself many questions. She did not wish to bother her parents and to add to their worries. "Why do the Zionists destroy their good life? Why do they come with these crazy ideas about the death of God? Why do they come with this idea of a Jewish homeland just to disturb my family? Do they know that Iraq is my motherland? What is the reason that the Chief Rabbi condemns Zionism? Who are those stupid teenage Iraqi Jews who built underground cells for the Zionists in Baghdad?"

Her mother had told her recently that the Zionists in Palestine have their women fighting in the fields instead of marrying and bringing children into the world. She heard from her Muslim girlfriends that the Zionists live in colonies and that they practice Communism. Her mind was filled with information, misinformation and propaganda. However, with every fire comes smoke or maybe the opposite. Saeeda trusted God but he did not seem to care for her anymore.

The first time she heard about the Kibbutz she was surprised that the word sounded funny to her. It sounded like constipation in Arabic. She smiled a lot every time she said the word out loud. Someone on the radio repeated the words Nakba (disaster) and Awda (return) again and again, expressing the view of Palestinians about the establishment of Israel. They did not dare to write or say the words "Israel" in the media. They preferred the term the Zionist gangs. The synagogues were suddenly filled with Hebrew voices asking Elohim-Allah for salvation.

There was no way to understand this Iraqi Allah. Saeeda was disappointed but not in a state of despair. Little doubts penetrated her heart about the logic of one heaven and God's cosmic silence facing atrocities. She wrote in her diary: "God does not act now because he does not wish to or because all of these terrible events are beyond his ability to control." She rarely cried but she felt that she was allowed to shed some tears now.

Her mother tried to consult the Darwish but it was never possible to locate him. This was in her view, a negative omen. Prayers did not help. "Why?" Saeeda wished to know. Many Iraqis did not know the answer either. She saw the thousands and thousands of Jewish soldiers arriving from the north, the south, and the center to leave Mother Iraq behind them. Circumstances were beyond their control. Saeeda's dreams remained dreams.

CHAPTER 4
Confession

Saeeda had been rejected by the mores of her culture: "Why do they hate women? Why are they afraid of them? Why do they write such beautiful poems about their mothers, their softness?" She had heard stories about men beating up their wives or even raping them but the women kept silent. In this culture women suffered silently because of the stigma attached to rape. Arab judges allowed abusive men to go free. Many men preached morality but they liked the honey of the women of the streets. Women were sex objects to be used, controlled and thrown away.

Saeeda never thought that these things applied to her parents. Her mother looked content and her father respected. However, she read papers and she heard the news. Saeeda was now 16 and no one could hide the truth from her. She needed at this age the pure truth, the absolute truth—not the truth of the adults which is measured by half, quarter and third measures.

So, some Jewish and Arab husbands were actually pimps. What a discovery! Jewish men refused to give the get to their wives, stranding them in the prime of their lives? Where was she before the discovery of these facts and events? Saeeda was convinced now that seeing all of these masses of Iraqi Jews assembling in synagogues in order to leave their beloved country had opened her eyes to see life! She was not as naïve as she was two or three years ago. She sensed things that she did not see. But among the masses of Iraqi Jews she saw all sorts: the doctors, the lawyers, the merchants, the thieves, the rabbis, the educators, the teachers, the destitute, the whores, the beggars, the primitive and the sophisticated.

Saeeda seeing the waves of Kurdistani Jews, the Baghdadi, the Basrawis, the Mosolyawis, the villagers from all over the Rafiden. had seen the beautiful, the ugly and the real. What a mess! Thousands of years were being packed up into suitcases by hundreds of thousands of Iraqi souls in order to be uprooted like chaff in the wind. Saeeda saw the sky of possibilities and the earth of reality in a few months: Suddenly furniture was sold for a few dinars; packages were tied with ropes and bye-bye Iraq.

CHAPTER 5
The Unpromised Land: Metamorphosis

The religious Jews in Israel refused to shake hands with her because she was a woman. Since you get your period, you are "unclean", they told her. They could not believe that an Iraqi Jew was rich, assimilated and had a decent life. She was seen as brown but the Jews who spoke with her had light skin. They changed her name to Sara because of the "s" in her name. "Saeeda is too Arabic," she was told. They were amazed that she was the only child because those who gave her shelter in the tent city assumed that all Iraqis took the commandment to be fruitful and multiply literally. They were surprised to learn that she spoke, read and wrote their languages. She was told about pioneers who come from Russia and Poland and built a state for the Jews, but she was lost in this strange history.

What is wrong with speaking Arabic? Their social worker suggested that Saeeda could work as a maid in a rich village until she could find a school and a house. Her father just sat down staring at the fabric of their tent. His biblical Hebrew was mocked by the Israelis. Her mother did not work for weeks because there were no showers in the dorm tents. There were also young Jewish whores in the tents. Like Saeeda, many of them were seamstresses, young wives and students in the past life of their birth place in the Arab world.

The women who came to help the Iraqi immigrant women were full of the feeling of performing an important mission. They came to teach Saeeda and others like her lessons in hygiene as if they never brushed their teeth in Iraq, as if they never washed their bodies in Arab lands. These women came with their D.D.T, their soap and their free thought about sexuality. They spoke about free love, they talked freely about orgasm, masturbation and penetration while Saeeda was embarrassed and ashamed of the words of these women. In her native Iraq, sex was left to the bedroom and to adults.

Saeeda lost weight dramatically. Her face dried and shrunk. Her body looked smaller now. Her eyes sunk further in their sockets. The first time she wore a pair of pants, it was bizarre and awkward. The zipper in the front of her private part was much like a man's! What was the meaning of this fashion? Girls wearing shorts and showing their underwear to boys. What kind of corrupt society is this Jewish State?

Many people worked on the Sabbath and smoked cigarettes on this holy day. Some even ate pork and frogs. This was a country of mishmash. Some people spoke with strange German and Hebrew accents that were totally alien to her ears. This was the first time she ever heard about something called the Shoah (Holocaust). When? Where? Why? This was the first time in which names like Herzl, Ben-Gurion and Golda had popped up from nowhere. She had heard about Socialists and Communists when she still lived in Iraq but she did not imagine that in a Jewish State you would find them controlling the state and superimposing their culture on those Jews who believed only in a divine redemption.

Life was a tent with non-stop rain and it had created a muddy mess. Cold penetrated their bones. Her parents had agreed to transport her to a place called a Kibbutz. In desperation, they wanted Saeeda to have a better life. They did not have any idea of what a kibbutz would be like. At the age of 17, she was introduced to youth, who like her, were born in Arab lands. A transition had occurred. Sara (Saeeda) began wearing the shirts of the Socialist left. She began singing praises to Stalin and his Mafia cadres. She was writing poems in Hebrew about equality between nations and about working based on your ability and being supplied on the basis of your needs. They loved Karl Marx in her collective settlement and other obscure Jews like Gordon Borochov and Berl.

She contributed her time editing the work of Meir, Yaari and Moshe Sinai. Everyone noticed her talent in writing. It was almost a miraculous event how she mastered the Hebrew language so rapidly. Her sexual desires were spent on her involvement in public affairs trying to bring peace and love to the entire world. Her parents were on a different planet now. She preferred to visit them driving a tractor from her kibbutz to the city of tents. She told her mother that her virginity had been surrendered to a nice, sensitive boy. Her mother just looked at her without reacting. Her father just stared at her with an empty look. The fire in them had been extinguished many months ago.

Saeeda spoke to them in Hebrew in front of her friends and in Iraqi Arabic when she was alone with them. She was embarrassed to articulate any Arabic word publicly. After all, Arabs were the enemy here and their language and culture were despised by many. She made every effort to hide the obvious: she was an Arab herself. Some Yiddish words began to enter her jargon. Some slang codes had replaced her cute expressions. She was ready to join the army of endless wars and victims. She, like other females, wished to show that the differences between males and females did not exist. She was determined to parachute from a military airplane and to join the course for the young female commanders. She also wished very much to be like all the Sabras. She loved the mythological story about native Israelis (Sabras) being tough on the outside and soft on the inside. After all, Sabra means cactus in Arabic. However, rudeness had often replaced toughness and the direct Israeli attitude has been considered by many to be nothing but chutzpah. She was living the myth and she loved it. Life was wonderful. She was doing something for the community. She used machine guns, she commanded over 60 female soldiers. She built up her body to be solid and muscular. Being a tomboy with short hair was a nice thing to be.

She believed in her heart of hearts now that the only difference between men and women is that the former can pee standing while women need to sit to perform the same task. In the 1950s no one had heard of the term feminist but who cared? She behaved like one of those radicals who see pregnancy as a male plot to enslave the poor woman. She made this change so quickly and so radically. She set out to prove that social conditions can shape a person and not her place of birth.

CHAPTER 6

With more experience and marriage, she was attracted now to the history of various regions. Self-centered and confident, she lived with him for many years. In those days, living together and producing children were the things to do. Marriage was considered a bourgeois custom which should be avoided. Boys and girls showered together and all kibbutz members came to eat in the dining room. There was no personal money and no personal materials.

The community provided modest furniture. Her clothes were sent to a communal laundry to be cleaned. With her intellectual curiosity, she read about the Trinity of the Christians. It was rather bizarre and confusing. God is one and three at the same time? The entire idea of God, she was convinced, is a human plot because of the irrationality in all of us. The world would be better without God, she often told her husband.

The small settlement began to look smaller with its same routines and same faces every day. Working in the field in the sun was fun for a while but not when one needs to get up early and work more than 12 hours a day, year after year. Her natural intelligence had begun to clash with her love of the secular themes of the Socialist Zionists of her time. She needed to breathe more and more. She did not regret her experiences and changes but it was time to see if there was a world beyond the barbed wires of her settlement which were placed there against Arab infiltrators from the Jordan River.

The army was incredible. Life and death had been intertwined—funerals of the fallen, fake and eloquent eulogies, eliminating those who come to terrorize Jews. "This place called Israel," she thought, "in her silent moments is like a surrealistic black and white movie with repeating occurrences of tragic events and incredible despair."

But, something went wrong. She did not know what occurred here, but she was convinced that something went terribly wrong here.

CHAPTER 7

The Kibbutz needed to send an emissary to bring the good news to many assimilated Jews about the miracle of the state. She was selected because there was no one who was as smart and articulate as she. She was burning with ideology and hope. No one knew about her doubts, but her own soul. With two toddlers and a husband who had served as the secretary of the kibbutz, she left to bring the revolution of the Jewish people in their land after thousands of years of exile.

She had practiced her American English and she studied about the ways in which affairs are conducted in American culture. She learned how to present matters in a polite fashion and to expect disagreements. She was told to smile a lot and to present facts in order to generate both money and sympathy. She needed to polish her directness and to learn to be more settled in her talks to skeptical Jewish and non-Jewish audiences. She knew that the Israeli topic was quite problematic but with confidence and trust in herself, she flew El-Al to the Big Apple.

She was eager and ready. She became almost professional after the intensive course in her homeland. She found it challenging to speak to independent Jewish students about the jewel of the East. Too many questions were asked about occupied territories, terrorism, and confiscation of lands, biblical mythologies, imprisonment, torture, and radical Islam. Questions about Zionism and post-Zionism were raised. This was too much to handle.

She realized that Israel had become some kind of Torah to those American Jews who cared about the struggling Jewish State. Exaggerations, misinformation, and emotional attachments have struck Sara Alon (Baghdadi no more). When she was asked about Arab-Jews, she related without exception the official line about the greatness of Israeli society that offered Sephardic Jews salvation, progress and goodwill. She knew better, but her job demanded the easy answer. Telling the real story about it would only raise new and embarrassing questions which would poke a hole in the Israeli balloon.

She knew how to change the conversation to the incredible technological achievements of Israel. This was basically true. However, she knew that one needs two to tango. The two sides need to be presented in this bloody conflict. She heard from the kindergarten teacher of her children that the former Zionist emissary had decided to stay in America. Sara Alon saw the irony. "Israel has been built on an irony," she said once. This gap between the training in Israel and the reality on the ground had begun to widen. She continuously smiled and answered questions with civility and humor. She learned the art of debate and she was generally liked as a person.

She grew tired of all the prepared speeches in synagogues and Jewish schools. Some interest and indifference was king these days. She knew how to keep her frustration for herself but at night when her husband returned from work in the Jewish Federation, anger and tears were not unknown in her bedroom. She was exhausted and depleted emotionally. Arab and Muslim students in some universities were openly and loudly aggressive. "Why is it that the world cannot see the official Israeli point of view?" she asked. "Is it the traditional anti-Semitism? Is it that 60 years of conflict have brought numbness to the heart? Is it the strategic changes in world politics?"

Her son Dani and her daughter Dinah have grown. They are cute and charming. They give her life joy and meaning. Very young children offer this excitement until they turn into animals when they are teenagers. Her mother always said that children will extract the liquid out of your bones and leave you dry. This trinity, The Iraqi Jew, the Israeli nationalist and the American Jew in one person can kill you.

PART II

Dahood

The Chameleon Messiah

By Dr. David Rabeeya

CHAPTER 1

I was always skeptical of preachers of all religions because they often believed their unrealistic lofty words. However one Iraqi Jewish rabbi has convinced me that he was saying all of this flowery language about God not believing in their content and effects. It was expected for him to say these unscientific and irrational words of the supposed acts of divinity because his people wanted so much to believe in the unnatural.

Hakham Dahood always wore his reddish tarboosh on his head projecting authority and distance but he was always in a hurry to remove it when he entered his brick house in downtown Baghdad. Those were the days in which Allah was a Sultan and his subjects were attentive to his silence. Rabbi Dahood had an impressive voice with a great knowledge of the languages of the two cousins: Arabic and Hebrew. He was never married; therefore rumors were triggered trying to explain this unusual phenomenon in his God-fearing community. He just ignored all gossips and continued to pray with emotional devotion every word in the prayer book and to offer mesmerizing sermons about this world and the hereafter.

Someone was ready to swear that he saw him riding on horses on the Jewish Sabbath. Another person made it known that he saw the rabbi kissing a teenage girl in the dark ally of his humble synagogue. There are even those who heard from others that they saw him standing naked on his roof during one of the deadly hot summers of Baghdad. No one could really prove these accusations but the rumor mills continued to spin around him.

When the cantor of the synagogue asked him about all of these episodes, he always answered in one monotonic voice, "I am always either in the synagogue or at home. Jewish people have a wonderful imagination. Let them dream."

He continued to pray with such devotion that tears frequently dropped from his brown eyes. His sincere voice of the prayers of the high holidays brought everyone to tears. One child ran to his mother claiming that he saw Satan wearing the tarboosh of Rabbi Dahood. A young lady swore on the grave of her mother and father that the Rabbi looked at her with a frightening look and as a result, she was struck by the evil eye and no man wishes to be near her.

Without any warning the rabbi disappeared and left no trace. His house was searched by the police and they could not find anything which would offer any hint about his whereabouts. They did find a black notebook with the names of various married women, the names of their husbands and occupations. Some joked in the community about the flight of the rabbi to heaven to meet Elijah and Emuck but some have taken these jobs quite seriously. The homeless guy in the narrow street placed his hands on the Hebrew bible to declare that the spirit of Rabbi Dahood visited him in his dreams and he is convinced that the rabbi is invincible like all angels.

In the synagogue, a new young rabbi named Haroon has just taken the place of the famous Dahood but when he tried to sing the melodies, the voice of Rabbi Dahood has come out of his mouth. Stunned and fearful, many members of the synagogue suggested calling the Muslim Darwish in order to perform the ceremony of the extraction of the Jewish devil from the body of Haroon. Dahood or someone similar to him was seen in the cemeteries on tops of roofs and in basements. Photographs of Dahood were dispersed in stores, factories and schools.

The Chief Rabbi of Iraq has declared publicly that those who call Dahood a messiah are committing sins and backlashing because the Messiah will come on time and Dahood cannot even meet the requirements of the Messiah. All of those talks about Dahood-Messiah need to stop immediately.

CHAPTER 2

In the synagogue of Basra, a man with a long black beard came to pray every dawn. No one asked him about his identity because the tradition demanded the acceptance of any Jew who wishes to worship the divine. He always sat in the corner of this house of worship and murmured words about belief, trust and hope. His voice attracted the people in his proximity. Sometimes he failed to appear everyday but he never missed the prayers of Saturday.

Infrequently they saw him talking with an attractive woman near the place of God. Her habit was to deliver to him a large sealed manila envelope. The stranger has introduced himself as Hikmat from the Kurdish city of Arbeel in Kurdistan. He knew both Aramaic and Syrian and some idiomatic expressions in Turkish and Iranian. He was wearing the traditional Kurdish cloth with wide pants and a large twisted hat full of colors and symbols. He was usually quiet in his demeanor, but when he talked he was able to attract attention to his words. It was difficult exactly to pinpoint his origin as if clouds were hovering of his head.

The cantor fell ill suddenly and he went to visit his creator. They offered the job to Hikmat but he insisted to be called "prince." When they inquired about his strange nickname, he told them that his ancestors belonged to the tribe of the ancient priests and therefore he needed to respect their heritage. The Arabic melodies of his prayers hit their hearts deeply. His dramatic gestures in the deliverance of his speeches were attractive. His words of wisdom about the invisible God have created disagreements among the believers but he handled all of these bursts of emotions with his diplomatic smooth language.

"God," he said. "Is an idea and nothing more." God, according to his concept is energy and he really cannot and would not get involved with everyone's life. Some were shocked, some have only smiled and some have even agreed but they did not dare to say it out loud.

Stories about his legendary power have spread in all of Kurdistan. It was told that he could remove people who envied others. He was supposed to eliminate jealousy, grudges, greed and ill will. He was the man who could deal with the evil eye and destroy it with his unusual power. They remembered that he always said every promise. He was amazing.

He convinced the Jews in the small and the large villages of Kurdistan that he can disclose the hidden meaning of biblical tests. Reckoning the numerical value of things was his thing. They actually heard him articulating the Tetraga numeration the four letters of God. They were fearful that Allah would be quite angry when he hears his personal name being pronounced out loud. When he was challenged about his belief in metempsychosis, he was ready to admit his trust in this doctrine. The passing of the soul at death will, without doubt, migrate into another body. He taught selected chapters of the Zohar and he amazed those who heard him about his memory and his incredible capacity to make mysterious matters clear and understandable. He claimed that he possessed a manuscript which was supposedly written by Elijah, the Prophet. No one saw this manuscript but his fantastic claims have only enhanced his unique personality. People love stories about miracles and he gave them both stories and unusual deeds in the metaphysical realm Hikmat is living here and nowhere.

CHAPTER 3

Then, he just vanished! Many people missed his mysterious charm and the many unknown things beyond him. Emptiness fell in the synagogue. His lessons were quite provocative. What kind of Iraqi Jew is this gentleman? Questioning God and believing in him. He had doubt about the divinity of the Torah and love with all of his might. Contradictions were his signs and symbols. He was rational, kabbalist, skeptical and devoted. He was a real character.

In the village of the Anbar region of Iraq, a wanderer Bedouin appeared near the tent of Sheik Ali the Great. His Iraqi Arabic dialect was totally Muslim in nature. He knew all of the rituals. He bowed down three times and kissed the hand of the sheik. He used many expressions of welcome with their ringing Arabic sounds. He wore traditional kafiyya on his head and with others he fell on his face to the ground praying the Muslim prayers with extreme devotion.

He asked people to call him Salman. He told a story about his Baghdadi family of Husseini who fled to Iran because of their refusal to leave their tent and to love in the urban complex of the capital. There were so many Husseini families in Baghdad and there were so many clans with this name. Salman was circumcised but so was the sheik. He was asked to tend the flocks of famous leaders in the tribe. They asked him many questions about his wife and children but in a consistent matter he always said that the regime in Baghdad has either killed them or they are lost in Iran somewhere. A man of great imagination, he told them about his wife Aziza and his three children Hamza, Jaafar and Khdeeja. They begged him to tell stories about life in Baghdad near the campfires of the desert. The more they asked him, the more he imagined even more events and occurrences. Why not?

His devotion to Allah was exceptional, which has added respect and reverence to his personality. Many unmarried women in the tribe showed interest in this handsome and sharp-minded man. He liked to measure women with his piercing looks quietly conveying messages of love and desire and expectations. Those eyes beyond the veils have driven him crazy. In his imagination, he undressed all these young women imagining their hidden physical maps of their delicious female bodies.

Salman seems to know how to talk to cows, sheep and horses, camels and goats. They obeyed his order murmuring unexplained syllables. He rarely used his stick. He preferred to play his shepherd flute made of word and cut from the yellowish and brownish trunks. His Arabic words and melodies combined love, separation, troubles and defeats into a beautiful and attractive voice. He loved singing and others loved his emotional expressions. Many have cried with tears acted by his sincere sounds and pleas.

Salman lived by himself in an old tent made out of skins of goats. The sun of the desert was cruel and demanding. Water was miles away in a small well. It was a harsh life but Allah always supplied food to his servants. His adopted tribe was involved in smuggling hashish from Jordan and Syria to Iraq. Nothing was wrong with this work. It was only a job which brought some dinars to the pockets. The skin of the animals was used to prepare tents and clothing. Most people walked barefoot anyhow and anywhere.

Salman knew many suras of the Qur'an by heart. Relatives of the sheik came to visit him from Kuwait. After the kissed on the cheeks and hugs, Salman walked with his herd into the storms of the dust and was never seen again. People were stunned. Since they were convinced that he died in the awful Khamsee, they considered Allah to be the decider as far as fate of the human in concerned. Someone came running from the far-away well to say that he saw the image of Salman in the water.

CHAPTER 4

The Church of Mariam the Virgin was located on a nice hill in the spacious green fields of Alwiyya the capital. It was a Catholic church in which the language of prayers was both Arabic and Aramaic. Antewan told the priest of this proud community that his family is originally from Syria and that he came to reside in Baghdad because of his involvement in the business of gems and pearls.

He preferred to be called Antony. The priest, a man in his 70s, asked him questions about Damascus and he was able to tell stories based on many geography books and atlases from his past education. He even mentioned the names of his Syrian priest in the suburb of Damascus. He needed to confess and Father George complied. Antony told him about his lies and deceptions of the past in general terms without revealing names and locations. He told stories about unlimited lust for women. Father George, detecting the Syrian dialect of his client, assured him that he will be forgiven by the lord.

A small contribution was left for the church and Antony never missed any Mass. Father George told him about Muslim youth who were sexually harassing young beautiful Christian girls. Father George loved Iraq and one could hear his nationalist devotion to the country of his birth but in the background was always sounds of apprehension and fears. He had many Muslim friends and many Imams from various mosques came to drink tea with him but the concern was always lurking in the background.

Antony came, prayed and socialized and his vegetarian excuses have spared him questions about his removal of beef, fish and chicken from his memories. He looked at the Statue of Yehashua with apprehension and curiosity. The eyes in the statue of the God of the believers have affected his capacity to pray. What about the Ten Commandments and the prohibition to worship statues? Well! He really knew the answer.

The statue is supposed to be a symbol of God. Case closed for him. Falling on his knees was strange and unusual but one can do whatever is needed to be visible and invisible at the same time to manage our common harsh life. He saw the Star of David and the Crescent and the Cross and he was not able to find out any hidden secrets besides the insistence of people to create legends, stories and scary feelings of guilt.

On one rainy day he left. Two policemen came to see Father George. There were some rumors about his involvement with a married woman in the church. He left stories which were told by members of his congregation. Some said he used to sneak out at night to have sex with young girls on the alter. Some said that they saw him walking at midnight dresses up as Jesus. Others just praised his generosity and prayed harder to find an answer. After all, his mystery is the mystery of the church.

CHAPTER 5

In the Jewish community of Baghdad, Dahood has been forgotten by many. However, stories about his mystical power still existed. An old-timer has expressed the view that Dahood may be the invisible Messiah of the Jews. Many have mocked this notion altogether, especially most rabbis of Iraq who have enough distorted ideas and thoughts about personal Messiahs. The Chief Rabbi has announced in clear terms that only God knows about the Messiah and signs will be sent from heaven to tell us about his identity. Until then, no one can claim anything. It is a dangerous game to claim to pretend and declare anything related to the son of David. Four or five false Jewish Messiahs in 3,000 years is more than enough.

The other false Messiahs are: Bar Kokhba, Shabtai Tzvi and Shlomo Molcho Shemenson. The local rabbi in his sermons has warned his flock. These charlatans with their disciples have created unrealistic expectations with a depression which always followed the false hopes. The Messiah will never sit in the gates of Rome or Baghdad. Its all fabricated stories.

Some soothsayers have prophesied that Rabbi Dahood has died but will soon come back from the next world. He will form peace on the entire world and bring all Jews from the entire world to the Promised Land. Some even dared to say that Dahood is still hiding in the basement of the synagogue in order to find meaning belonging to the shallow routine dynamics of everyday life. Some women went into sexual hysteria even when his name was mentioned but he is not there to witness this complimentary expression of him.

The elders have decided that the best way to stifle all of the crazy rumors is to establish at Bet-Din (religious court) in order to ban any belief in Dahood the Messiah. "He is dead!" they declared. They found two witnesses who were paid well testifying that they saw his body.

Dahood is watching all these human reactions from one corner of the narrow street only walking back and forth not taking any risk with any encounter of horny women. Dahood sometimes pretends to be a homeless beggar asking for alms. Dahood here, Dahood there, Dahood all of the time. Like his personal God, he changed places, spaces and spirits.

CHAPTER 6

Rumors have been brought to Dahood's synagogue about seeing him in mosques and churches. What does a non-Jew do in a Jewish institution? God only knows. The last piece of news was that he joined the underground Zionist movement in Baghdad with confidence. One congregant said that Dahood was tortured in jail and he was waiting to be hanged in a public place. Some women were wailing and shouting in the middle of this new tale.

One day in the desert of the dry Negev, a man dressed up in khaki appeared from nowhere. This year of 1948 was a year of decisions. Dahood has been smuggled in by agents of the intelligence of Israel. He spoke biblical Hebrew with a strong Arab accent and his knowledge of Jewish law has impressed the young Israeli solider. He had this untrimmed black beard which has added an impressive look to his brown face. His age indicted that he is from the reserve army trying to mingle with the 18-year old recruits.

He told them stories about his dreams about the unavoidable victories of the Jews in Palestine. He quoted verses from the Hebrew bible about Joshua, Samson, Deborah and David and their military defeats of their enemies. Most soldiers there never believed in God. They were skeptical; but his confidence did not hurt their moral. They were surprised that he had documents from the central military institution requesting his service with a group of mandatory aye soldiers. He obviously did not know much about weaponry but he knew a great deal about war stories from the bible. His presence was tolerated but these secular soldiers quietly admitted this encouragement was appreciated. He knew about weapons just enough to defend himself but he was in the age of actual fighting young men and wanted to fight. He was a skeptical religious man anyhow and he had many doubts about these supposedly religious texts. They are old, impractical and often cause wars and conflict.

However, he was a rabbi who was supposed to tell people the stories and tales because this is the oral tradition of Baghdad. Rumors about his unique power have amused him a great deal. Religion is supposed to entertain the people after all. God has a great sense of humor and he, Rabbi Dahood, is his agent. Rabbi Dahood was skeptical for everyone and everything and he liked it this way. His few comments about European Zionism were always short and sharp. Words like "unrealistic" and "beyond its time" and "more troubles than resolutions," were heard and ignored. He did not mind it.

CHAPTER 7

He met her in the reform synagogue of Beersheva. Opposites attract. She migrated from Russia and is older than him. She is a teacher of mathematics. She was attracted by his intelligence, charm and skepticism about the illusive things in life. He was unpredictable in his approach to God, Torah and the people of Israel (He called them the trinity of the Jews). She was in her 40s and looking for companionship. Her father was Christian and her mother was Jewish. She was a total non-believer. She was a Communist in her youth. God, in her view, was an idea in the mind-nothing more. Men and women need to believe there is something beyond the routine physical existence of the body.

She and Dahood have long discussions about being visible and invisible. She enjoyed all of the rumors about him. Dahood had told her many times that he liked to spread these rumors himself. He cannot even remember half of them. He knew that he was in many places but he cannot understand all of the fuss. Men can also come and go. The Messiah is a notion like all notions. It is all in the imagination and it is all illusions of the creative mind.

Her name was Olga but he called her "Olg" and she called him "Da". They were two intellectuals waiting to kill loneliness and defeats waiting for all. Da and Olg always looked for new adventures. They settled in the remote city of Yerokham in the burning desert. There were some Moroccan Jews who used to celebrate their own mythology about the survivor of the High Priest, the festival of Marmora and they were always in love with the graves of the saints. These psychologists and psychiatrists know something it seems.

EPILOGUE

He has heard the song, *David the King of Israel* in the Jewish Baghdadi suburbs but he laughed in his heart about the mythical David. Even in biblical tales, he is an S.O.B. womanizer and cruel like Satan. However, they wish to believe in matters of imagination. They place the word divinity in the bible and they began like blind sheep following a deaf shepherd. Even in Israel, they sing for the legendary king unable to find any archeological proof for his existence.

Dahood was not kidding. He meant every word. He read about so many people who told lies about their supposed power and they brought misery to many. The Messiah is a drug; it is opium that some Jews need to escape real life with its misery. He was like a lizard. He changed colors, fashions and beliefs ad places and nothing changed. Jewish Baghdad turned out to be an illusion like many other life's illusions. God of so many religions is like a thief disguised as a banker. "There is no reason to imagine anymore," said Dahood. It is far healthier to face the real picture.

PART III

A Novel

By Dr. David Rabeeya

PART 1
Aya from Allah

She believed in the power and the messages of her dreams. In her eyes, dreams were stranger than any realty. She dreamed in black and white and even in colors. No night has passed her without seeing visions and dreams. She was eager to sleep in order to see pictures and views with symbols, the horizon of the infinite. She saw almost everyone and everything. She saw the dead and the living. She even saw angels climbing ladders. She was just a simple uneducated woman from one of the slums of Baghdad. She was able to interpret the future fate of people on the basis of the traces of coffee in their empty finjans. She also frequently recited verses from the Qur'an in order to cure the mentally ill and those whose mind had left them altogether.

She wore these huge black dresses with fake precious stones on them. She wore blue rings in her ears and a green one in her nose. She used to collect the mud from the shore of the Euphrates to clean her hair. She was a great believer in the spiritual forces hidden in the mud. She also used it as a soap to wash her hands and legs. She was convinced that things found in nature could not be but positive with a healing essence.

Her habit was to collect fallen kernels from the stalks in the fields of the rich, and to feed herself and her chickens. Chickens then laid eggs. She was convinced that these chickens roaming in her cave in the vast desert of Allah were the healthiest chickens of her village. She never learned how to read and write, but her capacity to tell ancient stories was almost a phenomenon. She sang beautifully about love, death, yearning and the problems of humanity. She was invited to all weddings and funerals to sound her ululation shrieks. She was paid here and there and she always placed her meager income in an old handkerchief which was tied and tied again.

She had several names and she did not mind the observations and the remarks about this issue. She did not wish to explain the reasons. She was usually called Aya but she also answered to the names Aliyya, Fatma, Zainab and Khadija. Sometimes no one could locate her. She just vanished into the spacious desert with her skinny goats and sheep. She always returned cheerful and happy from these adventures into the burning hot gravel and sands as if the open space had added extra shots of life in her soul. She was married once but her husband left her for another Bedouin woman. He moved to the Jordanian desert in the West and she never saw him again. Aya did not mind that he set her free and he left her to take care of her business. She was aware then that a lonely woman in her tribe was considered dead, but her determination to live and dream has often overcome her particular situation among the Arabs. They needed her after all. She was a soothsayer and a dreamer and the controller of jinn. She was Aya, par excellence. After all, Aya is the holy verse of the Qur'an. How can anyone doubt her importance on this earth of ours?

Recently, she cured a mule which was struck by the evil eye. She took a stick of iron, placed it in the burning coals and stuck it in the behind of the mule. The beast jumped in the air like a demonic creature from hell. The animal shouted with miserable pain and then came a deafening silence. She twisted like a chicken after the knife has been placed on her neck. Quietness was in the air and within minutes she stood on her feet with a burning hole in her behind. She was surprisingly calm and obedient—relaxed that the penetrating wound had left her huge body. Aya continued to murmur gibberish Arabic words during this whole time.

Additionally, children with fever were cured by placing mud on their foreheads calling Saturn to leave their bodies. Barren women were asked to eat hazelnuts in order to remove their biological curse. Men with few hairs on their heads placed hot bricks with special incense on the naked area of their skulls. Some have sworn on the life of the Prophet that their hair miraculously grew anew. Aya delivered hundreds of primitive metal objects with Qur'anic verses to people inside and outside of her tribe. She was able to walk miles in order to prepare these objects. Her wooden hammer was able to flatten the metal and the primitive knife was able to cut them into pieces. She was seen visiting the grave of the holy man who, according to her tradition, was the first ancestor of the clan. She knew that people will believe whatever they wished to believe.

Aya had the habit to collect unique and unusual stones in her cave. People actually brought these stones and placed them in their pockets for good luck.

No one knew where she placed her income from her many functions and jobs. They saw her milking the goats, they saw her talking to them but her income was covered with secrets and rumors.

She heard about the big city of Baghdad, but her desert was the only home in her life. She knew that the city was in the West. She knew that Jordan was in the East. The sun and the stars were her guidance and this was enough. Aya could be noticed from a distance because of her tattoo on the top of her upper lip and her chubby body. She walked barefoot and she always laughed in her heart at those who wore sandals made of rugs and rope. She always believed that the flesh needs to touch the earth directly in order to feel the holiness of the latter. She claimed to move evil eyes and conflicts between couples and she never forgot to dream about them in order to solve their conflicts. She begged those who suffered to dream in order to find some comfort on earth. She was able to put herself to sleep by reciting some obscure words in Arabic and she knew in advance that dreams would follow her into the night. They saw her adding wood to her campfire during the blistery cold winter and then she also cooked her meal. Many rabbits and birds of prey were captured by her skills and she cooked them for her meals. A torn blanket made of the wool of some of her few sheep served as her bed. A huge stone under her head served as her pillow and it did not take her more than seconds before she swam into dreams and visions.

At night she covered the entrance of the gate of the cave with bushes and thorns. There were dangerous snakes in her cave, but many stories were told about her capacity to talk to them in order to leave her alone. Bedouins like to tell stories. Dramatic stories with incredible imagination and exaggeration were appreciated. From father to son, they told the same stories and every generation in her tribe just added and omitted to the first version which had risen from obscurity. Aya was able, according to some observers, to yell like the hyenas in order to chase them away from the village. Everyone feared the laughing hyenas because they can attract you to their caves in order to kill you and devour your flesh. It was dangerous to leave the tents, she once explained. The dark moon can bring unfortunate events in the lives of human beings, she claimed. They saw her bowing down with her forehead to the ground praying her duties to Allah five times a day. She was, without a doubt, a devout Muslim and people respected her love of the divine.

Most people of her village never forgot her conditions. They had less than her in material items, but their generosity was within their natural, cultural and social codes. She always thanked them while making physical gestures of gratitude. She looked at heaven and invoked the name of Allah, the merciful who will give them health and prosperity. Allah was invoked ten times everyday by everyone and she was not the exception to the rule.

She was thinking about her last days on earth but she tried to remove bad thoughts from her mind. She was not afraid of the unknown. Between her belief in her absolute faith in Allah and her fatalistic views, she survived well. She knew many verses of the Qur'an. She could read the text. She was able to recite Sutras and Ayas.

There were about a couple hundred people in her tribe and its name was Anbar. Therefore, she was known as Aya Al-Anbari. The Anbar tribe was a mixture of black and brown tribes whose members had migrated from Sudan in the Nineteenth-Century. They realized that they were the lowest hierarchy in the social scale. Aya did not care and did not know much about her remote past. She has placed her physical desire in the spirit of humanity. Her body did not feel the need for the touch of a man. She was content with herself and her destiny. The holy text has already stated that lack of patience in the work of Satan. Her patience was immanent and incredible. There was nothing to add. Being humble before Allah was her virtue. Helping others is her reason for existence. They are like herds of camels and cattle. They exist with the minimum because fate is not in their hands anyhow.

Aya has dreamed a new dream. Life goes on. Changes are rare. They desert always changes its forms and content but you need generations of men in order to recognize them. Some members were smuggling Hashish from Jordan to Iraq to add to their income but this is the way it was. Aya always said that the sand and gravel may fly by the storms of the desert, but man will always be around.

PART 2

Stories, Stories and More Stories

Aya found it very important to ask for all people in the tent village to come to the large bolder near her cave because she saw something in her last dream which affected every soul in her tribe. At the breeze of the evening, men came with their rifles and pistols. Women and children, according to the custom, followed them. After all, no one can call himself a man if he does not at least have a sword or a knife. Guns would be better but he needs to bring his manhood with him which is hidden in his weapon. She stood on the bolder silent like a rock. Her eyes were tightly closed and her face has shown unique intensity in her dry skin.

After several seconds, someone shouted words of encouragement basically asking her to trust Allah and talk. She offered sweet halva to a skinny girl near her boulder. She opened with the accepted religious formula of in the name of Allah, the most merciful and the most compassionate. Everyone repeated this mantra issuing their belief in the same Allah and respect toward the profound faith. Giant eagles will be flying soon in the direction of the temporary village.

She opened her eyes to see the hundreds who came to hear the news in her dream. They urged her again to tell them all details. Some have begged her to say it even if the messages are harsh and unbearable. Men called her "our sister" because these were the words of reverence to women outside their immediate family. She took several steps forward and touched gently the head of a toddler who had only rugs on his small body and said, "These birds of prey will seek flesh and they will tear their victims in minutes. Huge pipes with fire and smoke in them will cover the village with black clouds. Huge jumping frogs with steel and back will plow the desert and divide into small pieces. Many will die. There will be white canopies from the sky who will rest on the ground and fly toward the east and their color will be changed to red on their way to Baghdad."

She could see fire in the wells while many Arabian horses fell into huge holes in the ground. She went on to tell about the smell of poisonous gasoline in the rich thick air. People will run into caves but these cruel eagles will pluck them from within the caves and devour them in seconds. What could it be? One needs to ride through the desert to know about the glorious city of Baghdad.

Only selected messengers were able to cross these distances in order to bring the news from the capital. The messengers can meet whoever they can meet. They will hear the messages from various families, memorize them and retell them to their relatives in the village for payment. Furthermore, their village cannot be found even in old Turkish and British maps. They are here today, and tomorrow they will somehow be there.

She closed her eyes again and murmured some words of faith and rushed to her cave. Many words, idioms and sentences of religious devotion were expressed loudly by the audience. These expressions included praise to Allah, the greatest astonishment at his power in the universe and humbleness before his invisible presence. Women and children began to spontaneously cry not knowing if to fear or to trust Allah who can strike his servants on earth at his will and timing.

Aya then disappeared for weeks and no one could find her. When she came back they head her singing these emotionally-charged Arabic songs about lost love, cruelty, loneliness and struggles. Somehow singing about these themes has given her moments of total relaxation and peaceful existence. One could not have missed the deafening noises and sounds of the huge and monstrous airplanes that constantly buzzed her village and blew the eardrums of many.

Meanwhile, Aya continued to collect herbs from under the stones. In the small oasis nearby, she found some shrubs with medicinal qualities. She cooked and cooked again these dry brown plants on the top of one mountain to prepare her Bedouin medicine. She cared for those who could not sleep for fear from demons and evil eyes. She had also even offered a drink for stomach and joint ailments. She could stay for hours near the fire cooking her leaf teas and stirring water in her boiling coffee. These were hours of total devotion to deep breathing and silence. The sac made up from the skin of camels was always ready nearby. She drank a little because water was a rare commodity in the burning hell of the Anbar Desert. Some in the village were able to drink the forbidden alcohol from the nearby Qur'an, but Aya was not totally interested in the secrets of others. Aya knew a great deal of people's secrets because many came to pour their heart before her. They trusted her with their intimate secrets. Indeed, she never revealed any inside stories. There are no saints in Islam so she was just like a holy woman in the eyes of many. Some had four wives but they still liked the flesh of other women. Some were stealing chickens, cows, camels and goats from a nearby tribe. Some women had told her horror stories about awful abuse by their husbands. There is nothing new under the sun. Many people pray to God and destroy people.

PART 3

All attempts to convince her to leave have failed. She will go to the cave and die there. She cannot leave the graves of her ancestors in the vast desert. She cannot neglect her dreams in the semi-dark cave. She cannot leave forever the place of her birth. She wandered with the tribe a couple of kilometers here and a couple of kilometers there but she cannot accept the cause of the flood to erase her own sand and landscape. For her, not all corners of the spacious desert are the same. Some are really the place of death but some are the place to survive.

Tractors have arrived with their filthy smoke and dirty grease. They disturbed her sleep. She told everyone that the number of her dreams is decreasing. She saw people digging a huge hole in the middle of nowhere and she resented this act. Allah has strange ways to test his creatures. All of these monstrous machines with ugly teeth from steel were everywhere. Some members of her tribe have accepted through fatalistic approach the decree of the bosses of Baghdad but some have remained waiting for the miracle from heaven to change the orders.

Aya continued some indifference to her new situations of milking the goats and preparing delicious yogurt from it. She continued to remove the chaff from the grains and to back her pita in the oven of mud with yellowish and bluish fire without interruption. She refused to accept the unavoidable. She dreamed yesterday about burning fire descending from the sky and burning all machines. She also saw the image of her dead grandfather on the wall of the cave. She never prayed so hard and so intense to her silent Allah but she has told everyone that the lake will not reach her territory. She always felt relaxed with her cattle on the mountains.

She was thinking recently about her prophet Mohammed who used to walk in the desert waiting for divine interpretations and messages. She loved all large and small creatures in the desert: the wild gazelles, the hyenas, the huge lizards, the rabbits, the scorpions, the rats, ants and worms. She loved herself in the middle of her familiar reality and spiritual co-existence with the dryness and hidden life in holes and caves. She never raised her voice and she never shouted dirty words. She was frustrated but hopeful. "Water and sand cannot mix," she thought in her mind. One needs to seek waters not transfer them from one place to another. They have dug several times in the earth of her camp and they found some water. People did not want water. They preserved it and even the rare fast and little rain was a blessing.

This time many people in the village asked her to dream in order to find an answer to this terrible dilemma. Some have suggested facing the bureaucrats with rifles, swords and machetes. Some thought that staying there will frighten the administrators because they would not dare to flood the village and kill them with the gushing waters. Some were convinced that prayers to Allah will change the heart of the big shot in Baghdad.

The number of dreams has intensified and their messages became bleaker but tons of sand has been removed now. Dust was reaching the heights. The noise of the monstrous machine did not ever stop. At night, workers were digging while their light lamps were offering some rays. Some were measuring the huge hole in the ground. Some were pouring concrete by the tons to prepare the base for the coming waters. Someone has located Aya near the walls of the dam about ten miles from the village. There were some bones and some shreds of jars not far from the village. Aya's people were digging old statues from one hole in the mountains. Some were finding coins from Medieval Baghdad. Some were able to find pieces of old blankets and pillows in the dirt. They collected everything as there was no tomorrow. Some even found an old drawing with blood on it. Generations have buried and the desert was always consistent in his silence for thousands of years.

Aya cannot be found. Some elders went to see her or to be exact, find her. She vanished again but this time for a long, long time. Nothing in the cave indicated foul play. It has been already more than three weeks. No trace of the dreamer of all. Some were ready to bet on their only camel that she was taken by Allah. Some tried to convince everyone that she moved to Baghdad to beg in the dark street. Few assumed that she went to talk to the master of engineers nearby. One came with the idea that she was killed by the authorities because of her objection to the building of the dam. Everyone was upset because no one is there anymore. No one can replace Aya, the righteous of all.

Tens of Lories suddenly appeared out of nowhere. All rumors were prevalent; all hearsays were discussed in detail. One young Bedouin by the name of Azeez has sworn that he saw her face in the sky. A young girl with a suspicious reputation claimed to see Aya with the women of the night. They shrugged her comments and moved on. The soldiers with machine guns stood to answer any resentments or riots. Fear could be measured in the thick air.

Tunnels were built along kilometers and kilometers and it did not long until the sound of rushing gushing waters flowing from the Euphrates to the high dam ready to be channeled into tunnels. Plans for new cities in the desert have already been drawn on the tables of the contractors. A shepherd has been seen running from the field of shrubs shouting non-stop with hysteria the name of Aya, the matriarch. This was a frightening scene. He fainted and was rushed to and placed on the back of a camel far away from the original territory. Black and brown. The flood did not hesitate to cover what was the earth of the tribe. The traces of Aya could not be found this time. They vanished.

The flood has become a lake and the lake has connected to huge pipes. The beginning of urban complexity has risen with its yellow grass.

PART 4

The Collective Ayas

In the name of Allah and her faith, she began walking hundreds of kilometers in the cruel desert. She fed on cactus, wild potatoes and fruitful thorns. She knew the desert because she always survived it. She was able to defect into the barren mountains. The few drops of waters imprisoned between the huge boulders. She knew that she was walking west. The Northern star has always guided her in the long journeys with her animals.

There is no return right now. Her past has vanished into her memories of her old age. She loved her past and her dreams of events and fantasies. These visions have given her reasons for her constant wondering. Hope in Allah, the greatest of all Gods, is the way out of her new conditions. She never had any doubt that the merciful one will find a new way for her. It is difficult for her to imagine divorcing her pictures in the creative mind of a fine Muslim woman.

The skin on her legs has hardened in the oven of God. Her eyes became red from the musty storms. She covered her nose with an old handkerchief and places the kafiya on her head fighting the sharp rays on the red ball in the sky. She collected dry seeds and ate them intermittently. She was surviving. In the old nights she knew how to hit a stone against each other to start fires on the many dry leaves and branches.

In the caves, there were hyenas, wolves and foxes and poisonous snakes but it seemed they avoided her and she avoided them. She did not know how many days or nights or weeks she was walking in the hell of reality. She lost count but her dreams seemed to return. On one of those nights she dreamed about her camel and sheep being slaughtered by the police and eating their meat on skewers. She especially loved her goats in her dreams. She called them by names. She decorated their necks against demonic forces. The chickens in this dream have been cut to pieces and eaten by the animals and men. In other dreams she saw the sky opened with rain and floods changing the desert into a blooming meadow with flowers, trees and saplings like the paradise in her holy books. She was in paradise surrounded by streams, rives and water falls. The rainbow was so striking and beautiful. No houses were in her dream and desert. Only tents made up of the skin of sheep and goats.

When she opened her eyes, it actually started to rain. This was very unusual in this hellish place. Drops have fallen here and there, but not like this flood. She began climbing to the top of one of the high mountains to escape the awful and awesome irrational angry waters in her mind. Waters, like good and bad forces, are from Allah so why is she so angry about nothing? She was always convinced that no one can argue with Allah.

The way it started was the it ended. The rain has added a touch of green to the sandy earth. From afar, she saw a group of shepherds who in their features looked like a tribe from a far-away land. They were stunned to see an old woman dragging her feet in the sand with broken lips and sun burns on her face. They spoke Arabic but their pronunciation of words was different. She noticed this immediately despite the pain and agony of misery and loss. Her clothes were torn and her feet were bleeding. Like fine Bedouins, she was offered food and water and a place to rest in the tents of their women. Aya asked to call the wife of the Imam in the temporary mosque in the middle of nowhere. The mosque was just a small rug on the flying sands with curtains on top of it. Khatoon was her name. She was maybe Turkish or Persian.

Aya recited the Fatiha, smiled the smile of peace and tranquility. She was put in a deep hole somewhere. They covered the hold with more sand. Her grave just disappeared with the past. No one knew and no one cared because the monstrous change took over the world. In the computers of millions, the name Aya appears only as a name of a textual verse.

EPILOGUE

Every change needs to changed. We are all Ayas. God is only watching and he can only describe the change. Any questions? Dreams anyone?

PART IV

GOD

Interpreted/Misinterpreted

INTRODUCTION

The concept of God has always held conflicting messages. The purpose of this book is to unravel the misconceptions and mixed messages about God in monotheistic religions throughout history. More people have been killed in the name of God than for any other reason. Reflection upon man's manipulation of the concept of God under the guise of religion may serve the reader in his human journey.

God is always silent. People are always talkative. God has so many religions. People are convinced that their religion is the right one in our spacious universe. God is a commodity in the markets of humanity while he/she keeps his/her distance.

God is being manipulated by many and the eternal silence of the divine abuse continues forever. The monotheists often forget that they are in the demographic minorities of the planet. Most people in this world do not accept the idea of one god; therefore, new reflections of the monotheists concerning their negative utilization of the right God in their unique perspectives are due to be revealed to those who care about the divine defensive mode.

CHAPTER 1
The Illusive God

There will always be monotheists who claim that God has created the world. However, there are many who claim that the idea of God has been invented by humanity and that the entire concept is connected to the built-in human system trying to find any significance in their journey on earth.

The first group can even utilize tactical logical processes in order to prove the existence of God. The first logical assertion is that if there is a creation, there must be a creator. In other words, every picture was painted by an artist. The picture and the world did not just come into being without an outside power; the seemingly logical assumption is that the world has experienced a myriad of changes, catastrophes and violence, but continues to exist despite calamities and destruction by nature and man. Additionally, millions of people have lived and died and many have been born, but the unstoppable human cycles continue undisturbed for millions of years.

The third logical assumption is the existence of laws in nature which behave in predictable patterns and processes. The claim in this context is that some metaphysical power or a supreme being has placed them there for the survival of the universe and the perpetuation of laws of physics, which will guarantee the survival of the divine scheme. In addition, people of faith in the existence of the divine have also utilized their holy books: the Hebrew Bible, the New Testament and the Qur'an, to prove the miraculous revelations of these texts by a higher power placing them in a unique and distinguished position outside the realm of human literary creativity. For people of faith, God is the noun and the verb combined as well as the subject while people and their languages of communications constitute only the predicate concept of reality.

Religious people are puzzled by the process in which our world has formed into being, but they do not at all doubt the involvement of an outside and unimaginable energy, totally separated from human intelligence and emotion. God is unseen, but people need to seek him in their life knowing that he will constantly escape their perception and concept. For the believers, God can only be positive in his moral and ethical dimensions. Man, with this limited grasp of the divine, can only define him in a "negative" fashion. In other words, God cannot be "is", but "is not". The exclusion of all human characteristics from his essence can somehow offer some idea about his separated entity which is unrelated to the finite flesh and blood. He is infinite; was, is and will be! He is exclusive—unrelated to any human perspective and imagination.

Scientists may grant the religious people the freedom to believe whatever they wish, but they doubt their personalized concepts of God and their effect on their economic and political affairs. However, the ethicists may prefer to make value judgments about the people of faith, stating the dangerous actions and behaviors of the former toward themselves and others.

The religious symbol is often blamed for many bloody wars, massacres and intolerance in the history of human kind. It needs to be stated that many monotheists have always expressed some puzzlement about God's erratic behavior, but they often find a way to return to their basic faith. Through many generations they were able to find reasons, explanations and nationalizations to God's irrational activities and attitudes. Some of them have preferred to claim that the laws of God are not the laws of humans and, therefore, no one needs to be disturbed about the frequent clashes of these laws, leaving humans on the short side of the religious stick. Faith, according to this assumption, can always be tested; therefore, the acceptance of the contradictions needs to become an integral part of their absolute faith in the divine. Good needs to be totally trusted, even in times of tragedies, doubts and disillusions. Only absolute faith needs to be placed outside human events, even at the time of destruction and darkness. Sometimes the human argument is that God will allow suffering only to those who can tolerate suffering. He can never explain the holes in the theory of reward and punishment because often evil prevails and the goodness surrenders to the negative impulses of humanity.

The invention of negative human impulse and positive human impulse in a state of permanent conflicts has also been utilized to leave the onus of blame and guilt on humanity with the exclusion of God. In other words, reverence of the Supreme Being must transcend the wisdom which is the sole possession of God.

Many monotheists have also invented the hereafter to explain the success of many sinners and those who violate all or part of the Ten Commandments. According to this invention, God will reward the decent and righteous after their deaths. They also talk about themselves to elaborate in detail the demonic forces in Hell and the beautiful and serene description of Paradise. Sometimes Satan is brought to the picture in order to absolve God from any responsibility for man's evil behavior.

Since one cannot see or hear God, many monotheists have established names and codes to describe the indescribable. God has many attributes which are described in all parts of speech and the praises of the invincible are countless. Miracles real and imagined are attributed to the power that created nature and that controls it all. Some monotheists have always preferred to think about God as a personal God who actually can hear their prayers and requests. Some prefer to express the need for humanity, and to pray regardless of any assurances about deliverance of the request to the mysterious metaphysical power.

In general, it is rather not unusual for people to find God at a time of personal and communal troubles when many answers are unattainable and they have reached a dead end. It seems that the simplistic formula about expectation for messianic redemption at times of crisis has always continued to control people in dire need. Many religious monotheists have also perpetuated the belief about resurrection of the dead at the time of divine messianic restoration in the idealist world of the future. Some even convinced themselves that in the eschatological Armageddon war of the future, this world needs to reach its end in order for the positive virtues and righteous people to live happily ever after in the correct and pure world of the future.

A myriad of human images of destructions and redemptions have entered the faith of many monotheists in their attempts to find some order in this chaotic world of ours. It seems that human language is not able to express and comprehend the incomprehensible. Therefore, God continues to be the believer of a cosmic silence which in contradiction continues to make sense to them.

It is obvious that the journey to connect the existence and the activities of the mysterious God continues for millions of years and not many believers are willing to leave the endless trail to the unknown to new faith. The believers can offer expressions of awe and wonder to the incredible coordinated systems in the universe, unable to comprehend the depths of the endless space in the void. Stars also in the billions, planets of plenty and other heavenly entities are there to stay, to change and change again. The believers frequently look at the insignificant particles called human beings in the unlimited and infinite ocean of reality and imagination, convinced that an original creator has placed them there. They are destined to question about the meaning of the lack of existence before existence began to form.

Modern machines as well as robotic high speed computers are now able to penetrate the surface of many uncovered new phenomena, but are not able to find a common metaphysical formula to unite all existences into one. The human mind will always seek answers and some answers will be answered on tactical dimensions, but people continue to be puzzled by the strategic engineering structures and processes of all things together. The atom can be split now and the moon was conquered. Traveling to Mars is within the realm of possibilities, but after all inventions and discoveries, they remain as a drop in the unlimited divine ocean. The main argument of the believers is that we can place a drop found on the shore into the ocean but cannot take all of the waters of the ocean and place them into one drop. God only knows the believers explicit in nature.

Paradise with its promising flowing waters and virgin women may be interpreted in an eternal sense by many believers who may often prefer to see the sexual rewards as well as the other soothing phenomena in nature as an allegorical picture to accentuate the promises to the righteous. Hell is also dedicated in a blunt and no nonsense fashion about the pain and suffering of sinners. He is the ultimate decider about the tactical and the strategic movements of man. Therefore, people need to constantly praise him, fear him and be in a state of constant and continuous awe in relation to him. Every person needs to stand before him before his departure from Earth. Allah will judge severely the sinners and the righteous will receive their awards. The descriptions of those who are ready to die for the sake of Allah in the process of defending Muslims are the sharp differences between Paradise and Hell and have often brought hope and extreme fear into the hearts and minds of the faithful.

Islam believes strongly in the traditions of ancestors who carry the original religious precepts and their inspirations have derived from the Holy Qur'an which cannot be altered, changed or challenged as to its divine origin. The text may be interpreted within religious contexts, disciplines and methods, but not within academic principle utilized often in biblical criticism in the interpretations of Jewish and Christian texts in high schools and universities. Islam possesses the Qur'an (the holy written text) and the Hadith (the oral tradition). It is also a fact that Islam has several prestigious and influential religious centers and institutions which have tremendous influence upon both the legal communities of Muslims as well as the lives of many individuals of faith.

While many interpret the declaration "Allah Akbar" to be "God is great" (recognizing the greatness of God), there are those who interpret the word "Akbar" as placed within the superlative of the Arabic language, to mean "the greatest". One implication of this interpretation is that Allah of the Muslims is somehow superior to the God of others. Even those who interpret "Akbar" with a comparative linguistic context may conclude that, compared with others, Allah is a greater God than the others. The perception created is that Allah is the most monotheistic term which can be utilized to describe the absolute and supreme concept of the divine.

The intensity of the belief in Allah is demonstrated by many Muslims in their repeated utterance about the greatness of God and his determined involvement in their deeds. His name is uttered tens of times a day and he does not escape the literary and journalistic Arabic. Muslims cannot in reality utter strong or harsh words about their fate on earth and somehow the acceptance of fate needs to demonstrate the unshakable faith that God has his own reasons for our troubles and we can only trust his decisions and his judgment even if we tend to be baffled by what we think to be random divine acts of human suffering and misery. Indeed, shouting the name of God at times of troubles and insecurities has developed into an inner natural cry by many Muslims. This human need for God's help can sometimes be distorted by Muslim fanatics who utter out loud the name of Allah at the time of slaughtering their enemies and opponents during conflicts and wars. In this context non-Muslims often express disbelief that God's name can be invoked at a time of a blood shedding process.

The God of mercy and compassion can be turned by the radicals to serve as the God of vengeance and unusual cruelty, spreading fear and misinterpretation about the peaceful core of the Muslim religion. The cruel and inhuman methods of killing the enemies stand contrary to the peaceful voices of compassion and sensitivity found in the foundation of this religion. God of revenge and the settlement of scores often found himself outside the attributes of caring, protecting and nurturing, which are supposed to be the only virtues of one's supreme divinity. Some attributes developed from this disturbing contradiction concerning the nature of God to the Arab Bedouin ethos in the geographical Arab environments during the birth of their religion in the Twentieth Century. In other words cultural Arabism is still incorporated within the development of Islam since none of these atrocities are done by the same Arab Muslims of the Near East.

Historically, the massacres of Muslims by Muslims and the Massacres of Jews and Christians in the modern Arab states are both well known and documented in the annals of various Arab-Muslim regimes. The sincerity and the intensity of a sincere belief in God in Islam are never questionable, but the brutality committed by various individuals and groups in the name of God is questionable.

The genius of Islam is that it is willing to reconcile with the native cultures of non-Muslims in order to gradually convert them to Islam. The process of gradual Islamization of individuals while adhering to their former culture has enhanced the willingness of many to convert to Islam while continuing to adhere to their non-Arab culture. In the past, trade often served as an important motivator in these economic climbings of non-Muslims to higher positions in the society. Islam was even involved in the disintegration of the Feudal economic European systems of the past. Islam has always applied and extended its egalitarian religious concepts to the worlds of economy and finance. However, in Islam, justice has always taken precedence over freedom. Allah is in the mind and the mouth of many Muslims and the Arabic language represents this unavoidable will in Islam. Allah is very alive and very phenomenal.

Christianity needs Jesus in order for individuals to directly reach the Almighty God. Jesus needs to be the mediator and the agent of transmission in the process of supplications from the divine. Faith and theological dogma are the essential elements in the conception of God. Christianity without Jesus, who is the flesh and the divine, will become a religion of rituals lacking any theological legitimacy. After all, Christianity has come to remove the Commandments which are the core of the Jewish religion, and in allegorical ways, Jesus has replaced the Torah of the Jews. Many Christians continue to be puzzled by the theological doctrine of their faith in which God is one who can be expressed through more essential dimensions: the Father, the Son and the Holy Ghost (the Trinity). Jesus in Christianity has theologically come out to replace the sacrifice in the Jewish Temple of the past. Jesus now is the sacrificial lamb which has come to the world to sacrifice himself in order to absolve the sins of humans. It seems obvious now that Paul who has finally separated Christianity from Judaism was the major theological emergence who has faith, and perpetrated the major principles which have become the fundamentals of the new revolutionary religion. He was able to do this, against all orders to convince many pagans of this in the ancient world. The trinity has, according to some historical interpretation, fit assumptions of non-monotheists about gods and nature.

The assumptions concerning the influence of mythological Hellenistic concepts of Gods in the development of the mysterious trinity have already been considered by various religious and secular schools of thought. It also seems that the issue of faith minus the Jewish Ten Commandments has become a great source of the attraction of Christianity in the Gentile communities. No one can deny the incredible success of Christianity in the recruitment of believers and in the capacity to become the largest monotheistic regligion of the world.

In addition, it is within the theological nature of Christianity to extend its concept of God and the Trinity to the world outside its confinement. The Gospel needs to be exposed and spread to the world because non-Christians can see the shining light of Jesus the savior. Historically, Jews were usually the targets of Christian missionaries. Furthermore, it is well known that in medieval times Jews were also killed by various Christian religious institutions when the former had refused to convert to Christianity. The Crusades period can easily demonstrate the hatred and the violence against the Jews who wished to worship God based on their beliefs, traditions and texts. In the past, the inner contradictions between the preaching of love and care and the attacks against non-Christians have somehow blackened the image of Christianity as a religion interested in the humanity of God.

While one needs to emphasize the differences between Catholic, Protestant and Greek Orthodox, and others concerning the nature and the various customs, rituals and sacraments in the Christian religion, no Christian group can ever remove Jesus from the fundamentals of the religion. They may present various views about the theological formula "God, the Son and the Holy Ghost", but Jesus cannot be excluded from the core of faith. This doctrine may continue to challenge the idea of an indivisible distinguished and indefinable God. However, the power of Christian faith and convictions may lie in the absolute faith in a man (Jesus) who was converted to God. On the other hand, the images and statues of Jesus have sometimes been utilized to strengthen the need for people to visualize God in a human image. Additionally, the formation of saints in the Catholic discipline has also brought closer to the believer the constant need to evaluate their deeds, actions and thoughts in order to meet higher standards in the spiritual hierarchy.

However, this concept may also challenge the idea that God can interpret the crucifix as the symbolic representation of the one God. Jesus is so crucial to Christianity that he is being recognized as equal to God in the performance of miracles. Yet, here again a challenge will arise about the reconciliation between the miraculous mysterious nature of God with new and radical scientific developments in post modernity. On one hand, the idea of original sin has equalized all believers in their fragile human vulnerability, but also presents the view of the predestination of God in the view and judgment of his creatures.

Jesus who is prophet, teacher and God has confirmed in the Gospels that these theological combinations may add more challenges to the human-godly nature of Jesus, which can still be overwhelmed by uncompromised faith in being as God. The believers are convinced that they will rest with Jesus the God in the hereafter while others will be outside his grace and mercy. Faith can conquer all doubts and may be considered as a way to describe the powerful motivator in the Christian faith.

CHAPTER 2

Very few have religiously studied the theological history of Judaism, Christianity and Islam. The majority of monotheists who are born into these religions are unconsciously absorbed into them. Their faith is naturally identified with the religion of their parents; blending naturally into their immediate religious environment. It is true that some monotheists will either remain indifferent towards their faith or even skeptical about its principle, but the majority remain in their unique religious fold. Some will convert to other monotheistic religions (not usually applied to Islam), but generally most monotheists are born and die in their specific faith which was inherited by their own parents. Indeed, few monotheists have studied in depth in religious seminars and institutions as well as in academic settings the concept of God, the Book and Peoplehood within their particular faith.

Within this context, it seems that, together with their natural religious belief into their unique faith, they also developed consciously and unconsciously the notion that their particular theology transcends in quality and values the religions of others. It can be stated that in many ways the theology is most subject to many aspects of historical reality and national processes; every monotheist's religion offers its own suggestion about the absolute "truthfulness" of their unique understanding of God's intentions and nature.

Islam is convinced that the Qur'an constitutes the purest form of monotheism which has been revealed to correct and reconstruct the former monotheistic message of Judaism and Christianity. In this vein, Islam expects Jews and Christians to recognize their messages in the Qur'an itself. The Qur'an is the word of Allah where the Hebrew Bible and the New Testament are on the work of man. As a result, Islam, which chronologically appeared after Judaism and Christianity, has become in the mind of many Muslims the first and most accurate, original and divine text. This theological conviction of Islam cannot in any way be reconciled with Judaism and Christianity about their unique revealed text and its priority in the monotheistic scale.

After all, Judaism sees itself as the original religion which has invented the idea of monotheism. Abraham has largely become the personality who combined his incredible concept of Judaism and monotheism. In other words, in mythology, he has become the father of both revolutionary ideas. Islam considers Abraham the first Muslim (equal to be the first monotheist). Judaism is combining the two under one umbrella. Christianity has often claimed to inherit Judaism since the latter has surrendered its divine revelation to the former. Furthermore, the texts of the Hebrew Bible have been utilized to both project and confirm the words of Jesus. This theological Christian perspective has always created frustration and anger among many Jews because Jews wish to see their Hebrew Bible as a book which represents their religion and culture unrelated to someone else's religion. Jews have always rejected the use of their Bible as a vehicle to prove Christian religions and theological precepts and principles. Things become more complicated when the reality and the idea of God is influenced by the above disagreements between three monotheistic religions.

In Judaism anyone can search, argue and question God's decisions and activities. A person can also pray to him for assistance and help since God is both supreme and conveys the collective feelings, emotions, moods and intellect of all humanity. Judaism is impressed with faith, but it prefers to place deed before creed. In other words, the Mitzvot (the commands) needs to be at the core of Judaism and the personal involvement of the individual in correcting the evil in the world, which is, in the long analysis, the imitation of all of the noble and positive qualities of the divine. A few can become an atheist or agnostic in his/her approach to God, but they can still remain in the fold of Judaism since individuals have the freedom to decide for themselves about issues related to faith and God's existence. People can find themselves in difference positions in different phases in their life because altogether free will is considered to be the foundation of faith.

Judaism rejects the concept of dogma in religious affairs while it makes no compromise with the oneness of God. Theologically, the absolute obedience and surrender to God's will cannot be accepted in Judaism. Indeed, various Jewish schools of thought have argued about the defining silence of God in the face of tragedies and calamities by man and nature, and these arguments and questions cannot be stifled since the human mind has the liberty to end freedom and inquire about the reasons for God's indifference and the evils of suffering, wars and conflicts. Judaism sees itself as civilization in process with new dynamics which are needed to adapt to its new historical realities.

Indeed, the fresh evolvement and the new interpretations of the religious texts in light of scientific developments and discoveries must be included in the unending process of human growth. Within this context, the idea of God itself needs to adjust to tactical levels while helping the unchanged strategic commitment to the existence of our God.

Many Jews today have dropped the idea of a personal God as well as a personal messiah. Furthermore, only few still believe in the concept of the "chosen people". The majority of Jews have already accepted the notion that laws of history and nature have applied equally to all people, including the Jewish people.

Jews interested in Judaism continue to argue individually and through various religious movements about the essential ingredients of Judaism in the twenty-first century, as well as the need and practicality of many religious commandments in the secular changing world. Many question how the integrity and the triangle of God, Torah and the Jewish people are the sole theological aspects of Judaism. Some are questioning the existence of God as well as his existence in connection with revolutionary scientific discoveries. Many prefer now to emphasize the cultural aspects of Judaism as a living colonization.

The Torah is considered by the majority of Jews to be the foundation of Judaism, but its divine source is questioned now by many. However, the same majority has tremendous respect and love for the core of Jewish religion and theology found in the Torah. The fact that many Jews attribute the texts of the Torah to different human religious authors of the distant past does not affect the continual attachment to its laws and precepts. In general, there is awareness of the contributions of the concepts of the Torah to Western civilizations due to the utilization of the human and social messages of the texts in Christian communities worldwide.

There is no question that the words and voices of various prophets in the Hebrew Bible also have resonated in the minds of many Christian believers through centuries of competition between Judaism and Christianity. Today, some Jews even question if Judaism can stand on its theological feet if the belief of God is removed from the above triangle. Can Judaism survive only with the feeling of kinship among Jews from various diverse and ethnic cultural backgrounds? In addition, how can Judaism answer complicated bio-ethical issues related to ethical and moral dilemmas presented by modern medical technology? Also, how can Jews remain united in their theological principles when their common historical experiences are decreasing in quantitative and qualitative measures due to acceleration and assimilation in many diverse national entities? After all, Judaism today does not have a centralized religious authority which can at least suggest the principle legal Jewish decisions related to post-modern personal and communal life.

While one can always refer to precedents in existing Jewish texts in order to find some answers to complicated human issues in post-modern times, it becomes quite challenging to find possible resolutions outside the religious texts of the Torah and Talmud, and the myriad of commentaries about them in the thousands of years of Jewish existence. Nevertheless, the traditions of commentaries about physical and social, moral, economic, philosophical matters can open the door to new, original and unique challenges of modernity with its changes.

Many Jews today do not give any thought to the hereafter. In Islam, total surrender to God's will is the essence and the core of this religion. God, with his watchful eyes, knows and detects our actions in their details and punishes the sinners in the world of actuality and the world to come.

In many ways Islam leaves the fate of man in the hands of Allah. Allah can determine and navigate man's actions on earth and each Muslim needs to have total trust in him and his decision vis-à-vis humanity. In principle, not surrendering to God's will cannot be an option to the believer because the act of surrender must present the highest level of faith in the Supreme Being. God cannot be considered an idea or a thought which was invented by man because Allah cannot be an intellectual or physiological concept of the mind. He needs to be an entity, unrelated and familiar to humanity because of his distinguished domain and his capacity to bestow goodness on his creatures and supreme and sublime decisions to punish the evil in the world.

CHAPTER 3
Israel and God

With the establishment of Israel as a Jewish state various Jewish individuals and communities have developed a range of views about the theological and the religious meanings of the state. Some radical Orthodox Jews continue to principally oppose the existence of the state due to her establishment under secular Zionist foundations. Their insistence on waiting for a divine Messianic presence is both unstable and consistent based on their unique theological perspectives. Some of them will even participate with anti-Zionist organizations and groups calling for the dissembling of the state.

Other religious Jews reluctantly came to accept the Jewish state with its dominant secular orientation while reflecting the possible future separation between the state and the synagogue. They are willing to form political coalitions with secular parties in order to economically and financially benefit their members. They are aware of their political power in order to form a stable government. Therefore, they can often insist on receiving certain demands associated with budgets of religious schools, institutions, religious communal services, and the laws of the Sabbath, supervision of kosher food in restaurants, clubs and various exemptions from military services.

While the belief in God is maintained by many religious Jews, their involvement in politics is not unusual within their materialistic interests and political control. Their views about a state in which the Torah will become the belief in God combined within their Messianic dream is not of major interest of many Israelis who prefer to label themselves traditionalists. In other words, they are willing to follow the rituals of the Jewish religion due to social and cultural considerations and not because of any religious attachment related to the faith of the divine.

Most Israeli's prefer to see themselves as atheists or agnostics and they intensely feel that due to political consolation associated with unprotected religious power, they live under an oppressive religious regime outside the Democratic secular foundation of a modern state. They vehemently oppose the religious imposition of the minority of religious Jews upon the majority of secular Israelis. Many Jews wish to establish a constitution in order to protect individuals from the power of the religious political establishment. God, in their view, is used as a commodity in order to advance their exclusive earthly interests without any serious theological connections to faith and divinity.

Indeed, the majority of Israelis do not visit a synagogue. Many will not commit themselves to the Bar-Mitzvah and Bat Mitzvah ceremony. In reality, many Israelis question the validity of the divinity of the Torah's texts and they are also quite skeptical about the personal supervision over Jews. They are not expecting any redeemer called the Messiah to bring all Jews to the land of Israel, since they see this idea as no more than another mythological belief in an unreal world. God is not personal, if he exists at all, and Israel was established only because she was able to defeat the Arab armies in their attempts to destroy the Jewish state.

Additionally, many Sephardic (born in Arab and Muslim lands) Jews who believed in divine redemption are questioning now if their arrival in Israel was a divine act based on the scriptures. They believe after more than half a century in Israel that their presence in Israel was due to the War of Independence in which a huge part of the population was forced to migrate. Many Palestinians left Palestine and many Arab-Jews have arrived in the formative years of the state.

Ultimately, many Israeli Jews are trying to combine their Israeli nationalism with various levels of Jewish commitments in the realm of faith and rituals, skeptical of God's involvement in their achievements and crisis's. God may exist, but his influence as a real power in the incredible challenges facing Israeli Jews is another subject altogether.

CHAPTER 4
Israel and Christianity

Some Christians want Israel to be more Christian than Christianity itself. In other words, she is constantly criticized with their self-righteous tones about Israel's behaviors in the occupied territories, the status of the Arab Israeli minorities and the treatment of Christian missionaries by religious and secular official leaders of the Jewish establishment. They are often totally in denial about the natural establishments in a modern state which demand the building of the military forces and the protection of vital political and economic interests of the state based on strict national considerations.

In general, Israeli Jews are resentful of Christian missionaries who try to convert Jews to Christianity in the Jewish State itself. These activities often touched a nerve in the psyche of many Jews who were experienced in this religious position through their history in Christian lands. Another group of Christians are the Christian fundamentalists who are more Zionist than Jewish Zionists themselves. These groups of fundamentalists support Israel without any qualifications and compromises. They believe in the truth of the Bible (the Hebrew Bible as a vehicle to the New Testament) in order to predict the future restorations of the Jewish people in their Promised Land.

However, beyond their political and economic support for the Jewish state, one can easily detect their larger theological agenda with the intriguing entry of all Jews into Israel. Expectation for the Second Coming of Jesus will appear in a violent and decisive manner. The ultimate war between good and evil will take place and the Jewish people will see the light of conversion to Christianity and accept the man-God Jesus into their hearts.

Some Christian groups prefer to see Israel as an aggressive military state that has oppressed the Palestinians for many decades and the country needs to pay the price for her behavior. Symbolically, the Palestinians are the David of the struggle while Israel has been the Goliath of the world. Often, the complexity of the political and military situations in the Middle East is not of their specific interest because they are trying to judge the situation based on their subjective moral perspectives. God, according to these groups, is quite disturbed about the conversion of the Jewish state from a haven of righteous theological justification to a hell of disturbing reality. In light of this perspective, they prefer to punish Israel by economic divestment and the prevention of contacts with Israeli officials and institutions. Often, these groups have declared that their motivations are outside the realms of any anti-Semitic attitudes because they are trying to make their comments on the basis of ethical and moral considerations.

Some Christian groups were able to settle the theological and historical disagreements between Jews and Christians by recognizing Israel as a state among the nations of the world. The Vatican has established diplomatic relations with Israel despite pressures from many segments of numerous Christian communities in the Middle East and Europe, and despite concern that this act may be interpreted as a sign of equal theological values of Judaism and Christianity while traditionally Christianity has usually indicated her superiority and advances in the field. It is well accepted, for example, that the Catholic Church in medieval times and beyond has the survival of the Jews as an affront to Christianity, since the former have not seen the light in Jesus. In other words, Jews always insisted on rejecting Jesus as savior. They did not care if the church saw them as an obstacle to the fulfillment of the church doctrine in which the recognition of Jesus as God is the sole necessary way to seek salvation. The Jews prayed to God and they did not need any intermediary person-God committee with the divine.

Other Christian groups are supporting the Jewish state because of their conviction that the Judeo-Christian theology is an actual theological concept which needs to be preserved to counter Islamic attempts to convert the world to Islam. They see the rise of fundamentalist Islam as a global threat to Christianity which can be for tactical theological reasons a need to protect Judaism.

The reality is that many Christians of all denominations are very concerned about the rise of Islam and the conversion of Caucasian and African Americans to the fast growing religion. The "God of Islam" has begun to claim its superiority in various areas of the world, according to their views.

In conclusion, God and his usage and utilization in all monotheistic religions is for the sake of their own subjective interpretation of what God meant to say.

CONCLUSION

The God of the monotheists continues to shape and determine the developments of the culture and the history of many monotheistic societies. The gap between the idea of God and his/her interpretations by various monotheistic groups has frequently created instability, conflict and disagreement in the world. Leaving God to the individual seems to be a constructive resolution to this issue of faith and belief. Exposing the negative implications of the civilizations and ideas of God in established religions may exist in individuals. They wish to love and respect their spiritual trust in the unseen and the silence of these metaphysical forces in our lives. Let us give it a try again.

The idea of God in its purist sense can result in destruction, horror and devastation. Personal faith and belief in God needs not to be imposed on any individual since he/she has the right to ignore them all together. Each person needs to find his own personal God and his interpretation of the laws of nature and the universe. His faith must come from himself, not just from his parents and his legacy.

PART V

A collection of poems called
My Sephardic Muse: My History

My Sephardic Muse
My History

My Sephardic Muse
My History

CONTENTS

Genesis 99
   My Iraqi Genesis 99
Exodus 100
   My Exodus from Mythology 100
Leviticus 101
   My Forgotten Laws 101
Numbers 102
   My Many Numbers of Revolts 102
Deuteronomy 104
   My Third Jewish Deuteronomy 104
Epilogue 107
   The State of Israel 107
   My Hebrew Prayers 107
End of Illusions 108
My Biblical Commentaries 108
The Original Jew 109
Jewish Education in America 109
Some American Jewish Gaps 110
Jesus the Jew 110
Summary Circles 111
The Genesis God/Man 111
Time to Forget the Ancient Texts 112
Kaddish 112
My Hebrew Bible 112
The Story Beyond the Siddur 112
Who Wrote the Torah? 112
Israel: A Vision Delineated 113
Elijah's Fight 113
My Biblical Angels 113
Education Today 114
Love of God 114

My Invisible Bridge 114
My Round Small World 114
My Baghdadi Camera Eyes 115
Time Stood Still 115
Subjective Observations 115
Tent of Diaspora: Address Israel 116
Schma? 116
Shmone Esre 116
Green Branches 116
I am the Butterfly 117
False Images 117
On the River of Babylonia 117
Not a Dead Horse 118
Secret Wishes of an Iraqi Fighter 118
My Past Has Won 118
Ladders, Stones and Pillows 119
Baby at the Edge 119
Males from the Baghdad of My Past 119
The Israeli Syndrome 120
Iraqi Bread 120
The Key I Never Used 121
Jewish Baghdad No More 122
Israeli False Prophet 122

GENESIS

The Epic Journey of Elohim/Allah

My Iraqi Genesis

I was born with the brown waters of the Tigris flowing in my veins like the blue blood of my royal Hebrew mother. She was swimming with me in the Mesopotamian currents of the strong Euphrates. My father often jumped in the four rivers of Eden while I was formed in the fruitful liquid of the womb. The four elements of my childhood have affected my views of the endless universe. The land of Baghdad was like fruitful grains.

The air of the capital was at the breeze of the day. The light was warm, sweaty and with burning heat. The rich dew has always appeared between the black clouds. Streams of thought from past rabbis and academies have flown into my paths of lost and found files. The moon has often shown upon the crescents of the minarets. The stars over the stucco houses were always frequently larger than life. The rainbow over the Haroon El-Rasheed town has lit my colorful life's journey. After all, the struggles she has told me that waters will only heal. Suddenly, the storms of the hamsin have arrived all from the myths of the Promised Land. I could hear the whistles of bullets shrieking in the winds. Like the Tower of Babylonia, my Iraqi dreams have collapsed like dominos and cards. The synagogue in which my great grandfather has poured his tears and heart has flown into the thick air out of context. These holy manuscripts from the houses of life and death have been collected in a hurry from under the old walls. The Messianic eagles have landed in the dark nights of fear. I remember my wandering siddur, tifillin and Arab melancholic melodies on my soft shoulders and I fell into space floating without a base.

The sounds of the fall of the Iraqi waters have remained in my ears but my strong beautiful melody has never left me alone.

EXODUS

My Exodus from Mythology

These flying Arabian horses were galloping with me to the uncultivated land of my future. I run with all Jewish-Iraqi chariots to find the Sea of Reeds. In our visions, we stood in line to find the Holy Ark and the priests with their blessings. In our own imagination we crossed the horizon of the vast desert. We saw in our wishes the personal Messiah at the gates of Pumbedita and Sura. We have soared with our biblical verses like the birds to their secure nests. We promised ourselves all of the good wishes about the land of milk and honey. We danced our belly dances in our secretive chambers. Kurdish Jews were wearing the colorful coats of Joseph. I was ready and prepared to meet the God of the ancient Hebrews in his Jewish territory. The flight of the Cypress has lasted more than 40 Jewish hours but then the Golden calf was standing in my way to touch the Israeli Torah. My father in anger like Moses—the one who lost faith has shattered the tablets on the way to redemption. I read from the book of Psalms about the reward and punishment and I chuckled in disbelief. My mother began the dusting in the city of tents in a remote Israeli shore. We still had the strength to sing about the return to Zion by Ezra and Nehemiah and then we heard the lecture about fights, wars, victims and graves. My mother has already ripped out her hair like a Bedouin mourner in a depression procession. My father had not shaved before the imaginative Mt. Sinai. Like Israeli tribes of the remote past, we settled in tents in the barren land. There was no manna and no quire, only sand and gravel in our insecure uprootedness. I was an Iraqi-Jewish orphan who was asked to leave the orphanage. This time I climbed on the top of the Galilee and I saw the Promised Land on Mt Nebo. I had become the bearer of a defeated soldier like the Gibeonites of Mr. Yohshua. My Ten Commandments have been lost in the shuffle.

LEVITICUS

My Forgotten Laws

Unlike King Saul, I went to find a divine kingdom and I found only stubborn mules. My kosher lists have decreased in numbers. I hide my tattoo under my shirt. The verse of loving my neighbors has become only a text. Like the fringes of the Talit, I have scattered to the north, south, east and west. My Jewish-Iraqi tribe began with a strange accent. They have now placed the accent on the syllable before the end. Many sealed their Semitic mouths, hearing sounds and voices in a Judeo-Germanic dialect. My father lit all of the cigarettes in the Sabbath-ignoring his Jewish-Iraqi God in his exile in the Jewish State. I sang the songs and the slogans of Mr. Marx without knowing his records. I even pretended pathetically to shout and live these whining Hasidic melodies. While my lips were moving, my heart was bleeding. I had landed in a strange Jewish planet outside my Iraqi orbit. I constantly apologized about my Arab upbringing. You cannot be Jewish, I was told. I was only a teenager totally flying like a balloon in the vast sky. The army loved me. I was obedient, silent, but there was lava burning in my nostrils. I have taken the life of my enemy and he was an Arab. The blessing of the priest has been forgotten in my tent. I sang the Hebrew of Israel and quietly spoke to my soul in the Qur'anic tongue.

I quietly witnessed my parents who were withering like the leaves of winter. I was not bitter anymore. I preferred numbness to endure this hellish journey.

NUMBERS

My Many Numbers of Revolts

Like Miriam and Aharon, I challenged the power of the powerful human/divine forces. Why has Moses taken the lead? Is it because he was the prophet, appointed by God? Moses preached the Russian pioneer Torah of secularism and I was singing the blues of loss. Miriam was punished only because she lacked political power. I was convinced practical Aharon looked at me and understood my anguish. Moses was the radical monotheist with his particular ideology and his unpractical Platonic theories. My Jewish bones cannot be separated from my Arab flesh. I begged him. He demanded absolutism in the burning sun of the tent. Once in his sane moments, I quickly narrated my stories but not in his books with their cover ups and deception. Abraham was an Iraqi-Jew, I told him. He lived and breathed in my Mesopotamian earth. I am so young and tender, but very old in Jewish years. I saw the Jewish exiles-all the Babylonian prophets with their graves! Ezekiel, Naham, and Jonah among many anonymous others. I was the center of the universe. I inspected the pagans, the Christians, the Muslims and remained alive and well. I looked at the face of the Ottomans, the British and the Iraqi nationalists and continued to tick like an unstoppable clock. I built temples, hospitals, colleges and social and educational institutions. Even I was fearful of the eyes of the invading Bedouins of 1941. I knew intimately of these Jewish bodies hung in the flesh market of Baghdad. I heard of the electric shocks of the Jewish who rotted in the stinking jails. Iraq, the Arab was fighting Israel, the Jews and I am only an Arab-Jew caught between the histories of others who were dreaming the invisible dream about the Jewish messiah who will erase my pain in seconds. I did not care anymore about the lies and God's promises to me, about the Jewish land because the land I dreamed of was a land of so many sad realities. I looked at the calendars and the attacks were the same. The newspapers announced the unresolved dilemma. On land, two people locked in a swamp of memories, victimology and millions of my theologies and legends. I was Horah, the Jew, who has asked the legitimate questions, but the land swallowed him. I finally admitted I have lost the battle, but it was still going on in my inner soul.

DEUTERONOMY

My Third Jewish Deuteronomy

In this land of the free called the United many States, I have finally found my lost Jewish-Iraqi heritage. Here in this vast planet, no one knows about it and no one cares about it. No one can praise it and no one can put it down. I am like a fish swimming like all creatures of the sea against the current of the American many oceans. Here and there, some anonymous souls have accused me of being exotic and emotional. I confessed, to their total surprise, that I am a Jew. I did not wish to revise the truth anymore. I was eager to write my own version. In American suburbia, I am middle class, like many others. They always wish to know about my unique accent and I always say who cares about my past and your past. This is the land of the future. No one is allowed to live in the present. Things are rushing in the direction of the next event. Yankee Jews have been met with politeness and suspicion. Born in Arab Iraq, others were always intrigued but when I describe the particular individual Arab as human somehow, the walls of strangeness rise between us. Some are more Christian than the Pope when Israel is mentioned. Some only wish to speak about their Golda, B.G. and patch-eye Dayan. They throw into their mishmash English, some cute words in Yinglish and promise them with joy. I warned them against the repeated recitations of the discourses of Moses, the fantastic lover of God. I asked them to pay attention to the Exodus from Babylonia, where everything Jewish began. I spoke sometimes about Israel's flesh and blood, but they loved their unrealistic dreams. They live in time and I live in my space. I smile and I talk about the deserved punishment of Moses. He was so rigid, so disciplined that no Jew can follow his strict demands. My third version of the Torah was: Do little, but do it right. Many of them have made Israel, the Torah of the supposed chosen people. Some of them like to sanctify the land on the

East. They have these convictions about promises in vague divine verses. Some of them do not know what to do with stubborn Moses. They wish to be totally normal Americans without the burden of Israel's many faceted luggage. My neighbors speak so many French accents and ample amounts of cultural slogans. I am in this American human salad. Like gypsies, we come and go. I always rushed like them, like diligent ants back and forth trying to cover my body in a financial short blanket. I go to be present in a Jewish temple when ceremonies take place. I bring gifts like others and I even dance the old and tiring hora. I even sing with them the melodies of past European heritage. I am an expert in disguising my perspectives of these celebrations. However, I love being finally anonymous outside the communal definitions. The residues of past defeats will linger in my small apartment, but I will try to tell those interested only in the future; that my past will someday count in the annals of the silent universe. Elohim/Allah has traveled with me more than 70 years and his metamorphosis is noticeable in my complementary gestures in constant praise of him.

EPILOGUE

The State of Israel

A dream with a cutting covenant which has defeated the weak pagans. Molech is dead! Long live YHWH! The land was sprinkled with the divine Hebrew aroma. Elohim fought against his enemies with his holy ark. He placed his stamp on his land of sand, rocks and gravel and placed her in his heavens. He never asked his creature when he called it "The Promised Land." He has created the costly legend which burns us all.

My Hebrew Prayers

My lips are reading words but my heart is writing comments. Somehow my prayers have become grammatical exercises. The syllables, vowels, and accents are only cold, mosaic pictures. My body barely moves with the rhymes and rhythms, but my legs are made of steel and iron. At the end of it all, my indifferent cosmic silence conquers all. Like the Kaddish, no words can grasp my empty space.

End of Illusions

1967:
They were saved from the unimaginable but they fell in love with legends, sands and gravel in their expanded land.
Their Molech has demanded human sacrifices.
Golden Jerusalem has turned to prayers, to walls.

1973:
In their sleep the Pharonite soldiers have crossed the deep ditch with Qur'an and their faith.
The young Hebrew soldiers have succumbed to their drive.
Suddenly, the Messianic fervors have gone.

2009:
Besieged again by facts on the ground.
It is all obscure and predictable.

My Biblical Commentaries

I wish to collect all Midrashic texts into a huge pile in order not to find any answer.
I want all commentaries and exercises to be compiled for the sake of unknown intentions and profound silence.
I am eager to know how the original verses would react to their myriad of unpredictable explanations.
I have the tendency to scatter grains of salt and doubts on my skeptical tables in order for my intellect to solve nothing at the end.
No one really knows.

The Original Jew

I actually sat by the rivers of Babylonia waiting to see the man at the gate of Rome.
Indeed, the four streams of Eden were gushing in my veins.
Without any doubt, I climbed up the tower of Babel and I spoke in 70 languages.
In my child's reality I met Rebecca sobbing with joy at my well.
Adam, Eve, fruits and snakes were found in the walls of the house of my clan.
I remembered sailing with Grandpa Noah to find redemption on Ararat in the religious academies.
I witnessed waters flooding the reeds with the miracle man.
Suddenly, like the first mist of the creation, I vanished forever.

Jewish Education in America

If God would at least cover His madness with leaves.
If people would stop theorizing and do the brutal work.
If they would cancel all gifts to shallow Bar or Bat Mitzvahs.
If they would pray and understand a small percent of the Hebrew text.
If they would only become less self-righteous about their kosher food.
If they would stop quoting bombastic utterances by rabbis of old.
If they would only admit that they are Americans with the tiny letter "J."

Some American Jewish Gaps

They teach Amos and his bleeding justice but their behavior is as normal as others.
They quote rabbis in context and out of context and feel self-righteous about their income.
They build museums of synagogues and temples but the echo of empty chambers is in the air.
They fight over the customs of man in the name of the subjective invisible divine.
They wish to be Jewish in body and soul but they intertwine their blood with non-Jews.
They preach Israel from their roofs but they stay in the American Promised Land.
They see black clouds and they call them manna from heaven.
They despise talk about money and dues but they honor in their banquets those who possess the assets and the buildings.
It is an exaggeration but the seeds are true.

Jesus the Jew

Rabbi Yehoshua was one of those rabbis whose Judaism was burned into his inner bones.
He loved his people and resented their Roman bosses.
He was a Jewish patriot who stood against the establishment of his nation and the cruelty of the pagan Romans.
He died like every other human being and became dust and bones like all humans.
He left no mythology—only memories of fine human qualities.
However, those who needed a God of flesh and blood have haunted his divine aura.
They never asked him about this because he had already traveled to the grave.
His body was never found and it proved nothing to anybody because he was looking from the depths of mother earth, totally unaware of his supposedly divine qualities.
He was called so many names and he is just one of the Jews silent in a Jewish cemetery.

Summary Circles

The fights between the heart and the brain were constructive after all.
So many small victories and defeats.
Investigations through journeys were miraculous and refreshing.
Never a square but external cycles of new findings.
Joy and love despite it all
Faith may be shattered but living the intensive moments has confirmed my only and unique life.
Halleluhuman!

The Genesis God/Man

Friday God saw the world and graded it with "A."
Somehow he was able to ignore the burning light, the destructive flood, the splintering earthquake and the strong winds.
As a matter of fact, he was totally indifferent to the cruelty of the four elements.
He was pleased with his concept of goodness, but he could not prevent the human instinct to sin.
He blamed one tree in today's Iraq just to add excitement to the pain of free will.
Then he became generous and offered redemption to the weak of heart among his creatures.
At the end he admitted the obvious: We saw God and it is us.

Time to Forget the Ancient Texts

Billions of words on the ancient monotheistic texts without resolutions.
God never utters a word about their meanings.
Only man, the supreme being, has told his fellow man about their possible messages.
So much interpretation, reconstruction and manipulation in order to eliminate rivals.
So much hatred in the name of love in these impossible books.
New composers are needed to write some human texts from their inceptions.
God needs to sit quiet in the corner and allow critical people to write about the real, urgent issues.

Kaddish

I praised him beyond all words and then I was silent.
I could not find humanity in these lofty words.
Who is this entity who demands my entire attention and leaves me lonely in my bones?

My Hebrew Bible

My bible is only legends, tales and stories before history has been invented.
It is a sharp division between the non-real and the illusive mind.
I never met the authors to ask them about their meanings and intentions.
I have never encountered God to ask about the identity of the authors.
They made it holy without including the books which were to last forever.
If I needed to know about good and evil, I could easily watch my neighborhood to find them.

The Story Beyond the Siddur

Its words run through my eyes but they do not catch my attention.
It is only a compilation of thoughts, ideas and supplications of people like us who made thousands of attempts to find meanings for themselves.

Who Wrote the Torah?

Some nice influential Jewish men took kosher hide and pure ink and carved their legendary stories for thousands of years to come.
They wrote about their ups and downs as well as their legal life, fears and wars.
They looked for meanings and shared them with their YHWH of the Hebrew tribes.
They made Moses their only author and their God confirmed these many decisions.
In some chapters, they chose vague historical events and in others they created the world.
It seems that all geniuses can hear voices from within themselves.
The Torah has finally been delivered through their imagination and skill.

Israel: A Vision Delineated

She was always a state of mind as if she was built of castles of unpredictable dominos.
Like Jacob and his angel, she always limped with constantly bleeding thighs.
Similar to the shining, falling stars which have lit the darkness, looking for a place to land, exactly like the wandering bird which migrates everywhere and nowhere.
Her eternal syndromes are Samson, Masada and Bar-Kochba and they have left her in doubt like a female lover.
All waters cannot extinguish her doubt.
She prayed for thousands of years to fulfill a dream with one vision but she dwells in walls within walls for tens of years.
She is only a state of mind surrounded by those who refuse to recognize her vision.

Elijah's Fight

Elijah has flown into loneliness and vagueness.
He begged the imaginary chariots to return him to earth.
He found his promised heaven barren, without human sounds.
He took his superman dress and descended to earth, happy and real.

My Biblical Angels

They are flesh and blood in the biblical scrolls but the believers have flown them into their heavenly imagination.
They have forced them to divide into groups and ranks forming hierarchy in a thin air.
They have never visited me on foot or ladders.
They have never saved me from myself.

Education Today

If words could create the world God could not rest forever.
If new theories can be translated into reality, many teachers would continue to dig into the trenches with their severe challenges.
Since education is a business now, one needs only to buy it and elevate the grades.

Love of God

God never hugged me and kissed my cheeks.
He never listens to my critical inner thoughts about him.
He met me only when my desperation exceeded my frustration.
He wrote his emails to me under the delete regime.

My Invisible Bridge

In my sleep my soul conceived a bridge on the Tigris.
It was tall with plenty of steel.
My spirit came back to earth to rebuild it again.
Suddenly, Plato smiled at me holding the hands of his disciple Aristotle.
It seems that I saw a vision but my legs have actually walked on My Baghdadi Bridge.

My Round Small World

At sixteen my world was so linear.
I walked in it on the flat earth.
I felt the racing from beginning to end.
Then came real life.
Waters will become clouds.
Clouds will end with rain.
Mountains are in the oceans and dry land can be found any place in which the wind can carry it.
When I am home I long for far-away lands.
When I am in remote states I miss my humble, warm home.
The world is round after all.

My Baghdadi Camera Eyes

In the dark alleys of Baghdad I have left my memories jailed in the brick walls.
The blacksmiths with their hammers and yellow fire.
The tailors with their needles and strings on the Arab and European suits.
The carpenters collecting the saw of their sweaty chips and chaff.
There were also the secret beggars from the Iraqi police,
The ladies of the night with their reddish rouge on both cheeks.
I was walking to nowhere filming with my soft eyes the pictures of my future tomorrows.

Time Stood Still

In the dark mystery alleys of Baghdad, I have left my memories.
Those brick walls have closed on my spirit.
I walk, dizzy and longing for a world and many lives which were melted before my eyes.

Subjective Observations

The football gladiators and the capitol on the Hill.
The deadly competitions of the green in bloods.
The golden calf of the sellers of an obscure man-God.
The mass consumption of the flesh.
The people of the book on Google and AOL.
The empty walls of an ancient old God.
Master Card and Judaism pick and choose.
Left to right prayers with no roots.
Many preachers and few observers.
Futile arguments about non-kosher thoughts.
It is all up in the air.

Tent of Diaspora: Address Israel

My tent was opened to the elements.
My soul has closed her breathing windows.
My Arabic tongue has glued itself to my palate.
My Hebrew language has sucked in my lips.
Yiddish has been declared my foreign air.
My mother, like Lot's wife, has turned to pillars of lemon and salt.
My father has bent like a plucked feather.
My siblings were still removing their tears from the famous D.D.T
Finally, the picture of my tent is extremely visible on my sheets.

Schma?

Only when I fear I say the unavoidable Shma.
Only in my anxiety I recite it for everyone to hear.
Often I recognize it as a textual fabric.
Infrequently, I hope to find it redemptive.
Nevertheless, I admit that it is convenient to have around.

Shmone Esre

The prayer has changed the numerical concept.
She is eighteen blessings with a curse in the nineteenth.
They recite her standing on their feet like giving physical therapy to their bodies.

Green Branches

Like green branches who dare the snow to fall
I stood with my tree of life near the pools
Waiting for the branches to turn brown in their slow pace
Many trees have been chopped near my feet
However I stood face to face to the cold wind
Just anticipating the new green sprout
The rivers of Babylonia have never dried in my lonely forest

I am the Butterfly.

I always envy the butterfly on my door.
Rotting silent with his the color of the coat of Joseph
Aloof, proud and ready to fly whenever he wishes.
But no one has told me about the falls because I was so energetic with so many missions
I still like the butterfly on my door because he is still there
Greeting me everyday with his changing moods.

False Images

In the intersection of the Tigris and the Euphrates I met my young shadow.
Brown, erect and mischievous in my Joseph's robe
All the minarets were shouting to the silence of God
Distorted worships with weapons of faith.
I impressed them in my mind to be fearful in my life's journey.
My father was singing his naïve songs about exile in Babylonia
And I gave him my skeptic finger about his rosy Zion.

On the River of Babylonia

I always swam in the flowing rivers of my Tigris.
Watching the Baghdad Bedouins jumping to their death from my imaginary bridges.
I hung pictures of my streams in my walls of memories.
Drops of my Iraqi kindergarten still moisten my receding hair.
My wadi is gushing now with currents of Iraqi dust in Wayne, Pennsylvania.
No one knows and cares about my dry skins in the sun of my cold winter.
Only the Tigris like pure oil has anointed my soul.

Not a Dead Horse

My dead Sephardic horse died many times.
The eulogy was delayed until the hidden records were revealed.
No one is saying a word about his last noble race.
I can see him galloping in the Arabian desert,
Great and proud with his silky brownish skin.
He was so obedient to his alienated riders.
Once like the snake of Dan in Genesis,
His hoofs were bitten with poisonous milk.
I was once a horse like that
Waiting for the legend to revive me
To tell my story.

Secret Wishes of an Iraqi Fighter

I called strangers marrying my Mama the Big Papa.
I kissed and killed him at the same time . . .
The blood in my clay was never left in my veins.
It was spilled and gushed in the alleys of Baghdad.
I saw the lights of huge knives in many Iraqi windows.

My Past Has Won

I have tried to erase my Baghdadi past and that of compromised Israel.
I have tried to sleep through dreams of former visions.
I have forced my soul to think in numbers
Without any meaningful letters and symbols.
But the present tends to succumb to the memories of my past,
Refusing to live its own life in preparation of my future.

Ladders, Stones and Pillows

I have climbed with Jacob on the ladder to nowhere.
There were no angels and no demons,
Just thick air and my uncertainty about meaning.
There were no stones under my head,
Only soft pillows without my heart
Which was left in my beloved Baghdad.

Baby at the Edge

I was the child who was supposed to be killed by the sword of King Solomon the Wise.
My mother saved me from an imminent end.
The other mother lost me in the sand of dusty Ber Sheva
I have escaped all adult decisions
And I remain sheltered in a strange home.

Males from the Baghdad of My Past

I see Abu Dahood, the peddler of Indian grains and Chinese rice.
Abu Azoori with his black hat and Bedouin dress
Abu Yaa'gboob with his Fez on Thursday and tarboosh on Saturday
Abu Jamila who sang in weddings with his one tooth
Abu Hizgel with his brown moustache and black beard
I shall always keep their images in my wandering life.

The Israeli Syndrome

Every time she chooses one a new one pops up on the blurred horizon.
She tried the Samson syndrome to kill herself with her enemies like past Philistines.
She even contemplated the Massada syndrome.
We will eliminate ourselves by ourselves.
But the enemies will never catch us alive.
She tried the Bar Kokh syndrome where captured territories physically defend her.
She has the atom to blow herself to pieces and her enemies into small particles.
But she is never to find rest.

Iraqi Bread

My mother still bakes the Iraqi bread in my brick oven.
The thorns which enhanced the fire are still burning in my soul.
The aroma of the wet dow reach my nostrils on holidays.
How she placed the loaves like stars in a motherly order.
And how my father ate them with joy
And demanded even more.

The Key I Never Used

My Baghdadi G-d has come to rent to me my first apartment.
He was invisible, but He left the keys at the door
And I never saw Him again.
I could only hear Him in my crying childhood of Kol Nidre.
I had a glimpse of His invisibility
When I ate and blessed the Iraqi Jewish bread with the sour salt
On the eve of the Sabbath.
Once I even smelled His presence in the baking of the matza
In the clay oven
Torn into pieces while He enjoyed His silence
On the wings of the eagle to the Promised Land.
I have recited the Kaddish after His death
With the same Aramaic eloquence
Which He designed for His people.
Everyone has gathered at the Western Wall
To tell stories about His magical disappearance.
I wrote Him notes without His address
Until the dry wind burned those lovely requests.
One functionary spoke about the unseen lovely
Garden of Eden
And I had only giggled and laughed
At his thoughts and words.
I was told to praise His life
And to forget His demise,
But my burning tears have dried again.
Now I am hanging His keys under my pillow
Reciting the Sh'ma without mentioning His name.
Suddenly the entire blot of faith has been revealed
In my dreams.
He was, as usual, like many males
With plenty of muscles
Facing the women of His spirit.
The keys remain untouched.

Jewish Baghdad No More

The G-d of Genesis has placed me
Between Ishmael's moon and the sun of Abraham
The moon has darkened in its eclipse
When Jewish Baghdad died
And it has become a yellow grain in my Israeli cup.

I had walked between the cold rays
On the roof of Mt. Scopus
Waiting to observe the dim stars.
In despair I have tried to imitate the divine
By ordering the world's light to recreate me.

Suddenly my Arab flowers and my Jewish thorns
Have appeared in my reflective sheets.
I have enlightened myself
In the confinement of all poets.

Israeli False Prophet

He was called a false Prophet
But he continued his twisted visions and dreams.
They placed his predictions in jail.
His warnings in the politically correct syndrome,
His words were manipulated
In order to extract his sharp tongue.
He has told them again and again
That the pessimist is frequently right.
I was the false Prophet
Who stood on Mount Nebo
Shouting into the desert.
The Third Temple
Has completed its time
Consumed by fire.
No water to quench
My nightmarish prophecies.
I was truthful, after all.

PART VI

The Role of Resources in Middle East Conflicts

INTRODUCTION

People often take the existence of natural resources for granted as if their quantities will forever remain solid and not depleted. However, one can easily now detect more awareness of the looming crisis on the horizon of the world in general and the Middle East in particular. The economic interdependency of economic globalization together with the rapid industrialization of major new rising economic powers like China and India have made the Middle East an important region for the search=2 0for metals, oil, natural gas, and water. As a result, one can hear voices inside and outside the Arab world calling for military intervention in order to secure these resources when the physical survival of the national state might be jeopardized.

The Middle East constitutes not more than five percent of the population of the world, but the region possesses only about 0.9 percent of the global water resources which has led to the possibility of future political and social instability of this important strategic area. Indeed, few observers are questioning the slow depletion of the resources in the Middle East and North Africa. Many tend to mention the repeated external and internal conflicts and wars (ethnic, religious, tribal and national) which often result in mass migration as well as the decreasing quality of environmental factors (global warming, air and water pollution, contamination of soil, scarcity of fresh water, rapid industrialization, reduced quantities of metal, oil and water, deforestation, extension of desert areas and food shortages).

In the background of the growing problem of resources, one needs to mention the explosive birth rate in the Arab world of more than three hundred million people. These masses are in a continuous process of urbanization which involves the acquisition of household appliances, motor vehicles, electric appliances, etc. which urgently demand more natural resources which, according to some, are rapidly reaching a crisis situation. Channeling great quantities of water to wasteful traditional systems of irrigation has also put more demand and pressure on thousands of villages and small towns in this area of the world. This emergency situation is requiring us to find new sources of energy beyond what is used today. Indeed, the depletion of resources is placing more strain on the social and economic fabrics of many Arab societies which in turn can lead to military and subversive intervention for the basic needs of survival, in particular the need for water and an ample supply of basic foods. Famine, malnutrition and disease often have become byproducts of the general decline of the social qualities of some Arab societies.

All these factors need further investigation. Some Arab governments are pursuing several procedures and actions to ameliorate the difficulties of their citizens with regard to water and energy by extracting subterranean water and purifying and recycling dirty water and waste, transporting water from rich water countries like Turkey, upgrading and modernizing the irrigation and distribution systems and increasing the export of basic staples like rice, grain and beans from foreign lands in order to minimize the disproportionally large amounts of water directed toward agricultural usage and also the establishment of distilling water and using hydroponic methods of growing crops. In many ways the petro dollar incomes are being utilized in some segments of the Arab world in order to intensify the search for new quantities of water as well as in the investment of research.

WATER (TURKEY, IRAN, SYRIA, IRAQ, LEBANON)

In order to understand the looming crisis of wa ter in the Middle East one needs to mention two important facts. With the exception of large rivers in Iran and Turkey, all other rivers are shared by several countries which can explain the tension, conflicts and threats of war in their struggle to control the quantities of water needed for both their economic progress and the survival of their population. Furthermore, with the exception of the Nile, whose origin is equatorial Africa, the principal sources of water, springs, wells and rivers in the Middle East originate in this region.

Turkey is considered to be among the richest in water. The mountains of Armenia, with their high elevation and their rivers and snow and rain, supply ample water to Turkey. Plans to export water to various countries in the Middle East through pipelines have been considered intermittently despite the huge technical and financial investments needed for these projects. Indeed, Turkey enjoys plenty of water in her territory because of three main rivers within her borders: the Hizil Irmak, Sakariya and Ceyhan.

While the mountain ranges of Iran supply waters in many streams and rivers in the proximity of the Anatolian plateau, at the same time large quantities of water are being lost because they are absorbed by the salty marshes in the delta of Shat-El-Arab. Disagreements and conflicts over water have arisen between Turkey and Syria from 1980 and the two countries were at the brink of a serious military conflict. Indeed, despite the agreement of 1987 which is supposed to grant access to the Euphrates by Syria, the building of dams along the Turkish border, especially the Southeast Anatolia Project, continues to be a source of great concern to thirsty Syria.

Because Turkey, who is situated on the headwaters of the Tigris and the Euphrates, can easily divert, stop and decrease the amount of water channeled to the Syrian territory, the Syrians have found ample reasons to worry about the future of many parts of their arid and desert lands, especially after 1990 when Turkey unilaterally decided to fill the reservoirs in front of the Ataturk Dam. This action further slowed and diminished the current of the water to Syrian lands. The reality is that the repeated threats by Turkey to blockade the waters is leaving her on one hand almost in a veto power position over Syria's destiny and Syria, on the other hand, is often left to the mercy of others. Syria several times has contemplated waging war against the powerful Turkish army and its arsenal. It is an accident of history that Syria and Iraq are situated in the down stream areas of the Tigris and the Euphrates and they are obviously unable to change this geographical and historical position. It seems that even the strategic alliance of Iraq and Syria in this dire situation could not force Turkey to frequently ignore their pleas for the secure flow of water. Therefore, one should not exclude the possibility of a major war in the future over the refusal of Syria and Iraq to accept Turkey's dictation of the availability of the water needed for their survival. The Litani River is also in one country (Lebanon), but the amount of its water flowing to Turkey is limited and Lebanon is not able to supply all the water needed for her consumption. While Iran, with her Karun and Sufid Rud rivers, have direct control over the major sources of the country, there is an unresolved great amount wasted in her deserts. Dangers also arise in the control of rivers which cross the borders of several countries: the Nile (Ethiopia, Sudan, Egypt), Orontes (Turkey, Syria), Seyhan (Lebanon, Turkey), Jordan (Lebanon, Syria, Jordan and=2 0Israel), Yarmuz (Syria, Jordan, Israel). The unstable political situations in these countries (Syria's support of the Kurdish workers' party, genocide in the Sudan and Darfur, extreme tension between various ethnic and religious groups in Lebanon and the invasion of Kuwait by Sadam Hussein) have intensified the unpredictability of the actions of the regimes with regard to control of water, food and oil and the territories of their neighbors. After all, few countries in the Middle East are without desert (the deserts of Sahara, Sinai, Iraqi/Syrian/Jordanian and the Negev) and there is very little rainfall in these areas. These geographical facts exacerbate the acute situation of lack of water which can lead to desperate acts by some. Although large numbers of their population are still engaged in agriculture, while the development of modern and sophisticated systems of irrigation are in a continuous process, they are still not able to catch up with the demographic explosion of the population of their countries and this even further complicates the problems.

ISRAEL AND SYRIA

Israel and Syria clashed several times in the 1950s when Syrian forces made many efforts to prevent Israel from building its national water carrier. The building of this project has enabled Israel to transfer great quantities of water from the relatively rainy Galilee to arid areas in the South. This scenario has repeated itself before the Six Day War in the years 1965-66. Syria, again, tried to divert the water from the Jordan River into Syrian territories. Many political and military observers went so far as to argue that the fight over the water of the Jordan River was one of the principal reasons for the Six Day War despite the existence of other factors associated with the continuous conflicts between Arabs and Jews in the Middle East. Indeed, Israel's present control of the sources of the Jordan River has in many ways assisted the survival of the state.

In 1975 Syria tried to stop the flow of the Euphrates River to Iraq. Iraq did not hesitate to send troops to her border with Syria, threatening her with military actions.

ISRAEL AND THE PALESTINIAN AUTHORITY

Israel's continuous disagreements with the Palestinians over the issue of water has become a serious and unresolved issue for both sides involved in this conflict. It is a fact even in the Declaration of Principles signed by both Israel and the Palestinian Authority in 1993 they could not reach any agreement about the control of water resources.

The issue has a threefold perspective. First, the side that controls the summits of the mountains of the West Bank can divert the scarce water in her direction (Israel to the West; the Palestinians to the East).=2 0Second, The Palestinians have always claimed that Israel may surrender territories on the ground, but she will continue to control the major supply from rainfall on the mountains. And third the repeated disputed issue is the control of the mountain aquifer under the ground of the West Bank. This water is providing considerable amounts of water for agriculture in Israel as well as drinking water for the state.

The formula for equitable distribution of water does not exist. On the other hand, Israel has agreed to contribute some of the water of the Jordan River to Jordan on the basis of the peace agreement between the two countries. In 1994 their peace treaty contained an agreement concerning the distribution of water from the Jordan and the Yarmuk Rivers. On a practical level this arrangement came about to also avoid serious social and political unrest in the Jordanian kingdom due to the rapidly depleting quantities of water available to the kingdom.

In other words, in reality, no one can secure the continuous stability of the kingdom due to the demographic explosion of the Palestinian situation and its further demand on water and other resources for its survival.

EGYPT/ ETHIOPIA/ SUDAN

Many dams in the Sudan were built by the British when they were in power, especially those on the Blue Nile. The large Senan Dam was completed here in 1925 and it offered Sudan complete control over the water in this river. However, Egypt has extended her control over the White Nile. While Sudan and Egypt made an agreement about the waters of the Nile in 1950, Sudan has taken it upon herself to draw large quanities of water from the river by building two large dams (Jabal Awliya and Khasm al-Ghirba). Egypt, from her side, decided to build the giant high dam in Aswan in the 1950s with its large lake (Lake Nassar) in order to trap and store water in her terri tory. One by product of building these dams was hampered by the increasing amount of salt in the trapped water. This progress has resulted in new problematic by products.

For many years Ethiopia has registered her unhappiness concerning the allocation of water which was accomplished in the agreement of 1959 and, together with Sudan, has expressed their determination to start a military conflict against Egypt in order to increase their share of water. Egypt, in return, has always demonstrated her serious concern about attempts by Ethiopia to dam the Blue Nile. Since Egypt is situated in the downstream of the Nile, she has always been very sensitive about the motivations of the unstable regimes in Sudan and Ethiopia with regard to her survival with the water. The explosive demographic population has, again, made even the giant Nile unsatisfactory and unable to fill the needs for water in the area.

SAUDI ARABIA

Many observers agree that because of her location and geography Saudi Arabia is reaching a dangerous situation concerning the water supply which can wreak havoc on the social fabric of the kingdom. There are no rivers in the kingdom and there are no reservoirs of wells and springs. Furthermore, the kingdom needs to dedicate most of its deep well water to agriculture in order to guarantee food and food products to her people. This activity has often drained the deep water resources and polluted the few streams in the desert. Furthermore, exploitation of water in aquifers in the East has decreased the amount of water in Qatar and Bahrain. Saudi Arabia has invested billions of petro dollars in massive desalinization projects, but many agree that these projects may offer some relief for the short run but they are not able to resolve the problem for the long run. In any case, these projects have established a direct connection between oil and water.

Saudi=2 0Arabia and Jordan continue to argue about the distribution of an aquifer on their borders and this disagreement has poisoned the usually livable connection between the two kingdoms. The use of the petro dollar for the extraction of subterranean water with all its by products repeats itself in oil rich Libya.

OIL

According to some estimates the Middle East possesses more than thirty percent of the oil reservoir of the world and half of the world's phosphate can be found in Morocco. Many have observed that the control of the Suez Canal and the utilization of Arab oil and finding new markets for their products and goods were the goals of colonist powers of the past. The situation today is that many countries in Europe, as well as Japan, China and other countries including the United States depend partly or largely on the oil of Saudi Arabia, Kuwait, the United Arab Emirates and Iraq. While these countries receive some oil from Venezuela, Canada, Mexico, Nigeria and Russia, as the world supply peaks, it becomes more difficult to meet demands which places many countries under the threats of embargo, political blackmail and serious economic and social disruption in the stability of the universal economy. Indeed, the oil cartel of OPEC has accumulated serious political leverage over the oil. The Arab oil embargo against the United States in 1973 and the seizure of oil fields by Iraqi troops in their war with Iranian troops after the rise of the Khumeni regime, along with the invasion of Iraqi troops into oil rich Kuwait where Kuwait became a victim to Iraqi aggression, further complicated the stability of the area with its rich and coveted natural resources. Some observers even speculated that the invasion of Kuwait was a prelude to the Iraqi invasion of Saudi Arabia in order for Iraq to further its control of the resources in the area.

Most Saudi wells are near the Persian Gulf and the pipelines that carry the crude oil through Jordan and Syria to the Sudan and Lebanon are 1000 miles long and they were damaged by Palestinian-Arab saboteurs in Syria. The refineries in Saudi and in Bahrain are also in danger from the revolutionary Shite elements. Sunni Saudi Arabia contro ls the majority of the oil fields in the Middle East. Indeed, the Saudis were quite acute in their realization of this scenario allowing the armies of the "infidels" to save their kingdom and their oil.

Saddam Hussein also began to divert various streams of the Euphrates in the southern part of the country in order to dry up the area of the fruitful swamp lands as a punishment for their resentment of their objection to his regime. In the process, he created a serious calamity in the above environment which decimated the flora and the fauna in this area. In this context one needs to mention another factor in the destabilization of the region with regard to oil and the distribution of its rich revenues among the Arab citizens of the Middle East by its authoritarian regimes. The Kurds in the North of Iraq and the Shi'ites of the South have left the Sunnis in the central and the western areas of the country without any source of oil and deprived them from their economic and financial privileges at the time of the Saddam Hussein regime. Many have already noticed that ultimate political and social stability will be achieved in Iraq only when the Shi'ites and the Kurds will be willing to share the oil revenue with the Sunnis who lost much of their political clout after the fall of their leader.

FOOD

The rapid growth of the population in the Middle East, together with the rapid depletion of its resources, has also created a serious food shortage in many pockets of this area of the world. While the middle class has slowly begun to place itself in an important position on the economic scale, millions have remained involved in agricultural and manual work with substandard living conditions and low income and they are unable to adequately feed their large families. The ever rising cost of food and basic goods has made it difficult to purchase the necessary items for basic survival. One striking example to demonstrate this dire situation is that according to one statistic that more than 40% of all Egyptians live on less than $2 a day. Malnutrition, disease and lack of basic traditional staples such as cooking oil, rice, grain and beans fu rther add to the problems in this part of the world.

In order to prevent chaos in their land many Arab governments have offered generous subsidies in order to prevent violence, bloody revolt and internal chaos. It is always well documented that food supplies are also offered by countries and private governmental organizations in the West in addition to the United Nations who contribute both food and shelter to many refugees who are caught in the middle of the many conflicts in these areas.

CONCLUSION

Previous attacks by radical Muslim forces on oil fields and dams have increased the concern and fear about future terrorist activities in this area which ca n only worsen the economic situations of many common people with global implications for the economy of the entire world. Utilizing technological advances in the areas of flood control, modern irrigation systems and water conservation, present regimes are presently cooperating in strategic areas of common concerns, despite their previous history of conflicts and disagreements over resources and land. This may become an important key in resolving the issues and bringing about a more equitable distribution of the resources in order to assist in alleviating the condition of the masses and to prevent civil wars and famine in the area.

We have seen the results of the quest for control of vital resources in the faces of those refugees from Darfur and other areas in the region who are the displaced victims of those in power. This area's leaders need to change their focus to conserve and humanely harvest and distribute their water and oil to the many and the powerless, not to the few and powerful. The problem is urgent and real. The solution is urgent and global.